Courageously, Tess struggled to control her fear.

She would not look down—she must not. She paid full attention to her handholds on the side rails. Her lips felt dry, hands slippery. Twice, she paused to wipe a palm on her jeans before reaching for another higher rung.

Her head felt funny. Eyes closed with weakness and then in prayer, she leaned her head forward against a rung. *Dear God, please give me the courage to go on. I can't do this without assurance that You're with me.*

She felt a strong hand covering her right one and Pete's voice commended, "Good girl!" She looked up into approving brown eyes and, unbelievably, was able to smile a little bit. . . .

She moved her left hand to the right side of the ladder and reached toward Pete with her right one. To her surprise, he shook his head. "You don't need me, Tess," he said softly. "You're doing everything just right."

EILEEN M. BERGER is an award-winning author with over 100 articles, short stories, and poems published in popular periodicals. Her inspirational romance novels, *Lexi's Nature* and *Tori's Masquerade,* and her biblical novel, *The Samaritan Woman,* established her as an important Christian writer.

Books by Eileen M. Berger

HEARTSONG PRESENTS
HP18—Escort Homeward

ROMANCE READER—TWO BOOKS IN ONE
RR3—Lexi's Nature & Tori's Masquerade

A Place to Call Home

Eileen M. Berger

Heartsong Presents

ISBN 1-55748-410-4

A PLACE TO CALL HOME

PRINTED IN THE U.S.A.

one

Tess usually looked forward to the church dinners but she was forcing herself to go this evening. She told herself she would enjoy eating the delicious food and being with people she had known all her life. And she certainly needed a break from studying.

Hastily she spread peanut butter frosting on the german chocolate cake all the while hoping that the evening's program as announced from the pulpit and in this morning's bulletin wouldn't be boring. Peter Macfarland had only recently joined the church and seemed nice but she had had no opportunity to get to know him.

Her week had been awful and it didn't look like the next one would be much better. *I shouldn't have taken three major courses this term! I knew it would be a headache getting the Endowment and Special Gifts data to be compatible with the college's new computer system, but I didn't realize it would be this bad.* She liked her work and coworkers but—and what a big "but" it was—her major reason for accepting the computer job three years before was that she would be entitled to free tuition while completing her bachelor's degree.

She placed the cake into its carrier, not allowing herself even a glance at the textbook lying open upon the table.

5

She had been preparing all afternoon for tomorrow's test and deserved to relax for an hour or two.

The small church lot was filled so she parked her five-year-old red Honda halfway down the block. It was a gloriously beautiful October Sunday, the kind of day she associated with football games, walks, and drives in the country. The town's wide street was lined with huge maples, masses of red and gold, while the oaks had hardly begun to lose their brown, maroon, and dark yellow leaves.

Tess placed her cake with the other desserts on one of the long tables and joined the other people at those tables loaded down with salads, meats, vegetables, and breads. She filled her plate and found an empty seat.

Greeting those around her, she asked the tall, muscular man across from her, "When were you in Florida, Pete?" She understood he was to show pictures and tell of work he and others from his church had done in the Miami area.

"Almost immediately after Hurricane Andrew—from the twenty-ninth of August to Labor Day." His grin was boyish. "I barely had time for a few hours' sleep before the first day of school and a new classroom of twenty-four third-graders."

"What a schedule!"

"The rest of our group started back on Saturday, but I stayed till Monday. There was so much to be done!" His eyes wrinkled at the corners. He seemed to be looking into the past, seeing not this brightly lit Family Activity Center with about ninety well-fed and nicely dressed people, but the shambles and needs by which he had been surrounded in Florida.

"I. . .I think I'd have liked doing something like that," she said softly, pushing remnants of meat loaf around with her fork.

He leaned toward her, intense brown eyes holding her blue ones. "It's not too late, you know."

Tess drew back. "I really couldn't though—not now."

"Whenever." A slow, encouraging smile softened his urgency. "There are never enough volunteers, Tess. Nor enough time. And there are so many homeless people waiting almost despairingly for help."

A shiver passed up her spine. He was speaking of faraway things, yet he was looking deeply into her eyes and calling her by name. Before she needed to respond, someone asked him another question.

The tables were cleared, chairs rearranged, and Pastor Jim Hadden introduced the speaker of the evening. As Peter Macfarland had been here less than two months, some might not have had the opportunity of becoming acquainted with him. Pastor Jim explained that Pete had recently moved to Fairhills to teach in this school district and was especially interested in history, science, nature, bowling, and softball. And tonight Pete would be sharing accounts and pictures of his experiences while with people from his home church in Connecticut.

Tess couldn't help smiling when a teen on her right said, "I wish he was my teacher!" The girl next to her agreed. "He's really handsome!"

Yes. He is. Tess had been aware earlier of his easy smile and manner, his slightly wavy hair a shade lighter than his friendly eyes, and those muscular shoulders and arms emphasized, not hidden, by his open-collared, short-sleeved cotton shirt.

As he acknowledged the introduction, she realized how comfortable he was with his tallness and with being in front of people. He had grown up, he said, in a town and church about as large as this, the oldest of three children, and with all the kids on the block spending their time at his home.

"Perhaps," he said, "that's one reason I've always planned to work with children when I grew up. And why I'm enjoying this opportunity of having your third-graders in my classes."

He smoothly made the transition to telling of the trip to Florida. As soon as they saw TV coverage of Hurricane Andrew, several members of his church decided to go on a work tour. Their enthusiasm spread—so much that they filled two vans and Pete volunteered to drive a truckload of donated lumber and supplies.

Part of his program was presented on video, for he had ridden and walked around in Florida with a camcorder as well as his still camera. "As you can see," he pointed out as he panned a particularly hard-hit district, "there are entire streets where nothing was left standing and others where the damage was so great that nobody can live there.

"Those having insurance coverage are by now on their way to getting back to 'normal,' if there is such a thing in an area this heavily damaged. However, although the government's doing much to help, for many the wait for housing has seemed interminable."

He told of his reluctance to give so much time and energy in August, when major transitions were taking place in his life. "I might have backed out," he confessed, "had they not needed an experienced driver.

"As it happens, in order to help pay college expenses I'd worked in a lumberyard and driven trucks during vacations and, when my schedule permitted it, during the school year. The owner, a member of our church, offered one of his vehicles and wholesale prices for lumber and supplies if I drove.

"So," his eyebrows raised as he shrugged, "I found myself in Florida for what turned out to be one of the most unforgettable, exhausting, and blessed periods of my life." He then challenged them, "I understand some of you are active in prison fellowship ministries, scouting, and working with the aging or handicapped. These are worthwhile and if you truly have already full schedules, I'm not suggesting you add more.

"However, for those not so involved, please consider sharing time, energy, and financial resources to help those desperately needing what you have to give—your love."

His last words made an impact on Tess and stuck in her mind. She had no opportunity to speak with him after the presentation, but as she left she saw him look toward her over the heads of those crowding around. Her hand raised in a small salute and his head cocked slightly, as though in question. And he smiled.

When she arrived home, she put away the few pieces of dessert then changed into pajamas before getting back to her studies. After one more review of her notes, she decided she knew the material and, tired as she was, would benefit most from a full night's sleep.

Morning came quickly. She arrived early for work and stayed until ten minutes before her eleven o'clock sociology class. Afterwards, as she sat alone, eating the lunch she had brought from home, she checked through her book for underlinings and information written in the margins. Had she missed anything important?

She felt fairly confident when she entered the early afternoon psychology class and was relieved to find that the test was straightforward and direct, without the ambiguities and slanted questions the teacher had used the last time.

Tess returned to the computer department where she stayed late to compensate for class time. On the way back to her apartment, she bought a hoagie at the Kollege Korner. With fruit and milk it made the supper she ate while relaxing in the recliner watching the evening news and reading the paper.

She turned off the TV and was reaching for her textbook and notes on early childhood education when the phone rang. "Hello?"

"Hi, Tess, I have a message for you," said the masculine

voice.

"And a good evening to you, Pastor Jim!"

He laughed easily. "I usually do introduce myself when phoning, but it didn't seem necessary with you. So, how are you?"

"Fine, thanks. And you?"

"Okay. And now, as to my message: Pete Macfarland just called. He'd looked in the directory and called the operator to get your number—"

"Which is unlisted," Tess put in, as though it didn't matter that the handsome young teacher had tried to reach her.

"He discovered that, so he asked me to give it to him."

"Did you?"

"Of course not—though you might not have minded this time. You two seemed to be having an interesting conversation over dinner."

Was that a question? "The people at our table got a preview of his later presentation. He and I had never said more than 'Good morning' or 'Hello' before, but I enjoyed getting to know him."

"He's very personable," Pastor Jim agreed. "And a bachelor. And he likes you."

"Because he asked for my number?" she asked. "He probably wants to follow up on my saying I'd like to do something like he did. . .but I also said I wouldn't be able to."

"Could be, Tess." The words might have indicated he agreed, but the tone wasn't convincing. "His number's

555-4421, so you can find out when you call."

Tess hesitated. "I. . .really don't like phoning men."

"But you're the one who's unlisted. "

She sighed, knowing she was too curious about Pete's call to not check. Pastor Jim spoke of the dinner the evening before and, as she was on the Board of Christian Education, she and Pete also discussed a situation in the junior class before they wished one another a good night.

She sat with the phone in her hand for a time before punching in Pete's number. The receiver was lifted on the first ring and she said, "This is Theresa Kenneman. Pastor Haddon just told me you wished to speak with me."

"Hi, Theresa, or do you go by 'Tess'?"

Of course he would have heard others calling her that. "It's always 'Tess.' I don't know why I introduced myself like that." *Probably because I was uncomfortable about phoning.*

"I appreciate your calling. I want to thank you for keeping the conversation going at our table last night. You helped immeasurably in my getting to know people in a new place."

She smiled in the privacy of her apartment. "I was genuinely interested so the questions were mostly for my own information."

"Anything else you might want to know?" His voice sounded friendly and warm.

There was a lot she would like to know—about Pete. Pastor Jim had just said he was a bachelor, for example. But it wasn't proper to ask personal questions. "What kinds of things did you, personally, do after getting your lumber delivered?"

"Mostly cleanup. Backbreaking heavy work of cutting up and dragging trees and gathering trash—and that often meant all the furnishings and treasures that had made these places home. Digging trenches, putting up scaffolding, and replacing shingles on roofs that weren't too awfully damaged."

"That would be satisfying."

There was only a moment's pause. "How serious are you about wanting to do something like this?"

She had been afraid he would ask. "I am interested, Pete, but there's no way I could free up that much time in the foreseeable future."

He didn't say anything right away and she rushed in words to explain about the computer mess throughout the campus and specifically in her department. "It wouldn't have been so bad if things had been done in a logical fashion, instead of the administration's announcing that by a certain day everything will be switched to the new system.

"Until now, each department kept its records in its own way—and for the most part this worked fine. However, the people setting up any of these methods had a great deal of freedom. You can't believe the bizarre and original ways similar problems have been attacked."

"Sounds challenging!"

"To put it mildly! I'm in charge of getting several systems on-line—mainly everything that has to do with gifts of alumni, their families, corporations, and things like that."

"I don't envy you!"

She thanked him for his sympathy, then briefly explained that she had earned her associate degree in computer science and had been employed by an accounting firm before coming to work here. She was now taking as many courses as possible each semester toward her degree in early childhood education and counseling.

"I'm impressed!"

Considering the schedule she had been keeping, she felt justified in advising, "Don't be. It's probably a form of insanity."

He laughed. "If so, it should be contagious." But then he became more serious. "So what else do you do?"

She laid the textbook on the floor, not wanting to look at it. "Oh, there's church and Bible study, and I enjoy reading, and I sometimes go to dinner or a concert or something with friends."

"Am I 'friend' enough for you to consider dinner with me? Including a concert or anything else you'd like, of course?"

She did not respond with a definite "Yes" or "No" but afterwards she wasn't sure exactly what she had said. Something about seeing him at church next Sunday.

Why didn't I come right out and say I'd love to go with him? It was next to impossible to involve herself in the assignment for the following day. She unwillingly kept remembering their conversation. Given the opportunity, she felt he would ask her to go to Florida if a group went from here.

And she couldn't spare the time. She really couldn't.

It was on Wednesday, while she was making a tuna, lettuce, and tomato salad, that he called again. "Hi, Tess. Pete, here. Going to Bible study tonight?"

"Hello, Pete," she responded, wiping her hands on a paper towel and balancing the phone between her ear and shoulder. "I was planning to go. Are you?"

"Um-hmmm. Thought I'd try it tonight, and remembered you said you usually go. Can I stop for you?"

There was no reason to refuse. Not that she wanted to. "It may be out of your way—I'm on South Elm."

"How far out?"

"Seven-three-three."

"No problem. Look, have you eaten?"

"Not yet. I was late getting home again, so was in the process of making a salad."

"Can it keep till tomorrow?"

"I. . .I suppose so."

"In that case, how about my coming right away and we can stop at a restaurant on the way to church?"

Why not? "That sounds like an excellent idea," she agreed. "At the moment I'm wearing pants, sweater, and joggers. We're not very formal on Wednesday evenings. Should I change?"

"Depends on where you'd like to eat. How about the

Midway Steakhouse? I've never had a meal there that I didn't enjoy."

"I like it, too. When will you get here?"

"I'm leaving in about thirty seconds. Barring the traffic light's turning red at the wrong time, I should make it in under five minutes."

It was nearly six when he arrived, although if she had not looked at her watch she wouldn't have believed it. She put the salad in a sealed container and quickly straightened the newspaper, books, and pillows.

She had just finished putting a touch of color on her full lips when she heard him at the door. She shrugged into a lightweight jacket. "You made it through on the green light."

"Just." His eyes sparkled, enjoying her comment. "I saw in my rear view mirror that it was yellow by the time I passed. Now," he said, placing his hand beneath her elbow as they started down the walk, "perhaps we'd better make sure we know where we're going."

She glanced upward. "I thought it was the Midway."

"Only a suggestion. Is there a place you like better?"

She smiled. "The Midway will be fine."

After placing their orders, they helped themselves at the elaborate salad bar. They were soon seated opposite one another in a maroon upholstered booth with the soup, bread, fruit, and dessert they had chosen.

They were halfway through their meals when he asked, "Why are you smiling like that?"

"I didn't realize I was doing anything unusual."

He reached across and covered her left hand with his. "Not unusual, Tess. You have a lovely smile, as though you'd been given a present or something wonderful had happened."

She looked at their hands, then back up at his face. "I'm going to have to be careful, Mr. Peter Macfarland, if you read me this well."

"Then it is something good?"

She nodded. "I just realized we were conversing comfortably. I think that's good."

He gave her hand a firm squeeze before letting it go, but his eyes didn't release hers. "I agree. That's very good."

They did not speak again of things that could be taken too personally. Rather, they talked about the church and how Tess had grown up in it and had many special memories of the people and things that had happened.

He told of his playing varsity basketball in high school and being involved with track. "I wasn't an awfully good student in those days," he said. "*B*s seemed plenty good for anyone and I couldn't understand why my folks weren't satisfied with that especially when I could get them without studying."

"Being very intelligent can sometimes be a handicap."

"It can be—and was," he confessed. "My first job involved holding a sign telling motorists whether to stop or to go slow around road crews—and I was proud to be making more money than a lot of kids graduating from college."

Pete grimaced with self-deprecation. "It took me longer

than it should have to realize I wasn't going to be satisfied doing something like that for the rest of my life."

"That's when you returned to school?"

"Um-hmmm. And I held on to my job while taking night courses at the community college for several terms. Up till then I hadn't been motivated to save money."

"And you got all As?"

"And I got all As," he admitted. "With a lot of studying, I must add. It was worth the effort though, for I was then eligible for grants and financial aid. With that, my working at the lumberyard, and getting loans, I made it."

"I commend you." And she did, knowing from experience how hard it was to work and go to school. She shifted to a more comfortable position as she changed the subject. "How did you happen to come to our town?"

He leaned back in his seat and said thoughtfully, "I'd expected to get a job in my own area, but for two years my only teaching was as a substitute for various school districts—and that is far from being ideal."

She knew this to be true. "The financial crunch has hit schools systems here, too. As teachers retire or quit, many districts choose to have larger classes and part-time employees, rather than to hire replacements."

"I resolved to try many places and your school apparently liked my resumé well enough to have me come for interviews. And here I am!" He looked pleased with himself, or the situation, as he added, "So, in answer to how I got here, I'd say this must be where the Lord wants me."

Elbow on the table, chin resting on her loosely clenched fist, she smiled. "I like that—your giving Him the credit."

He smiled at her approval. "And you, Tess. How does that concept fit with your situation?"

The piece of steak she had lifted an inch or two above her plate was set back down. "Most of the time I've loved my work, and it's given me the opportunity to get additional credits toward my degree. I prayed for guidance before coming to the college three years ago. It seemed the right choice then and it still does, although right now, with this computer system mess, I have to keep reminding myself of that. Thanks, Pete, for making me remember."

It felt strange to enter the church with this man. She noted raised brows and nudges and knew that some were reading too much into this. She had never "brought a date" to Bible study before, so they were probably jumping to conclusions.

The pastor and others greeted Pete and some mentioned his presentation at the dinner three days before. By coincidence (Tess corrected her thinking to providentially) the Scriptures being emphasized that evening were those of Jesus' commending the giving of even a cup of water in His name.

Her hand started to reach for Pete's in recognition that his work in Florida had been like giving gallons of refreshment to thirsty sufferers. She drew it back in time, hoping nobody saw her gaffe.

At the door, when he brought her back to the apartment, Tess said, "Good night, Pete. I have pages and pages to study yet this evening."

But his smile and voice kept coming between her and the words of her book.

two

Pete wasn't at Bible study the next week and she saw him at church only in passing. *Have I offended him? Why hasn't he called?* She thought in confusionn. *Well, I don't have time to worry about him or any other man!*

Most of the secretaries were cooperating well with her as she strove to get the computer systems in conformity, but she was still exhausted by the stresses of her job and the long hours. What conceit had made her think she could engineer this technical transition and handle three courses besides?

She considered dropping a course, but which one? She was learning a great deal in each and actually looked forward to attending classes.

She disciplined herself to concentrate on every word her instructor spoke and refused to let anything interfere with study time. Each night she activated her phone's answering device and fastened a notepad on her door for messages.

Weeks flew by. Shortly after getting home from church and changing clothes one Sunday, Tess frowned at the ringing phone, annoyed with herself for neglecting to switch it to automatic. Wiping her hands on one paper towel, she protected the receiver by holding it with another. "Hello?"

"Hi, Tess. It's Pete."

She sank down onto a chair. "Hello. How are you?"

"Good, thanks. And you?"

"Messy, actually." There was humor in her voice. "You caught me in the final stages of stuffing a turkey for tonight's annual Church Family Thanksgiving Dinner. Are you going?"

"Wouldn't miss it. That's why I called. Can I pick you up?"

It sounded delightful. "Sure. And you can carry the roaster, if you wouldn't mind. It will be bulky, with this twenty-four-pound giant in it and being hot from the oven."

"It would be my pleasure."

The words were almost formal but his expressive voice made her believe he really would like to help. "Great. And if you manage that, I'll bring table service for both of us."

"Fine." There seemed the briefest of pauses before he said, "Well, I'd better not keep you from getting Big Bird into the oven. Shall I come about five-fifteen?"

"Perhaps a bit earlier? There has to be time to carve the turkey once we get there."

Five o'clock or a little earlier was the decision. Tess left the phone off the hook as she hurriedly finished preparing the turkey and getting it into the preheated oven.

She studied until four-thirty before changing into brown wool pants and her new gold sweater embroidered with autumn leaves. She brushed her long hair and fashioned it into a flattering french braid.

"Ummmm. I like!" he admired.

She wished he would make complete sentences. Not wanting to assume more than he meant, she indicated the sweater. "I couldn't resist buying it when I saw it at Lawry's recently."

He touched her hair. "The color's a perfect match."

She led him to the kitchen, turned off the oven, and let him lift the roaster to the stove's top. He removed the lid to admire the turkey. "Done to perfection!"

"I hope so. It's larger than I usually roast, but according to the directions, it had plenty of oven time."

Everything was wonderful with the evening—food, fellowship, being with Pete—everything! She especially enjoyed the surprise presentation.

Tess was in the kitchen drying dishes and assumed Pete was helping fold and put away the extra tables and chairs, but he wasn't around when she finished her work. Pastor Jim was missing, also.

She was visiting with several elderly women when Molly Eckers, chairwoman of the Social Committee, thanked everyone for coming and hoped each had had enough to eat. The response was a chorus of affirmation, made up partly of mock misery groans of those who had eaten too much.

Molly asked everyone to be seated so the evening's special guests could be introduced. Tess found two chairs together, laying her purse on the second to save it for Pete.

The door near the rear of the big room opened, revealing

two clowns. The tall, bold looking one with moplike orange hair wore a loose fitting outfit of white with huge multicolored polka dots and wide ruffles at the throat, wrists, and ankles. The second was probably as tall, but he wore oversize work overalls with varicolored patches, held up by one over-the-shoulder strap. He looked around, afraid of the place and the crowd of people.

Tess laughed out loud, recognizing Pastor Jim in the orange hair and Pete under the white face decorated with exaggerated worry lines and a huge down-turned mouth. Pastor Jim pulled Pete forward, silently miming reassurance that he didn't have to fear coming to the front of the room.

Molly verbally asked questions and said words to which Jim exuberantly responded in mime or by digging into his ugly purple plaid sack for boldly printed signs that he held up for all to see.

Pete hung back, trying to hide behind a supporting pole at center front then fearfully peeking between the spindles of a cane-bottom wooden chair. Molly included him in the "conversation" with firmly direct questions he "answered" by drawing from his ragged burlap bag first a hammer and large nails then, as appropriate, a crowbar, some shingles, a piece of torn tarpaper, and a road map of Florida, the lower portion of which was circled in fluorescent red.

Shoulders shaking with sobs, he cried silently into a torn red bandanna. He indicated the problem by huffing and puffing Molly's papers until they fell to the floor and then he blew a paper roof off of a Lincoln log house, which he also partially destroyed.

He cheered up though as he pointed to Pastor Jim, Molly, and himself and, with an all-inclusive sweep of his arm, to the audience, he mimed their going to the Miami area with tools and supplies to repair damage from the big wind.

By Pastor Jim's "driving" with Molly behind him and Pete in the rear, they showed they were going in a big vehicle to southern Florida and indicated they needed time, muscle, and money from the people in the church to make their trip possible.

When near the exit, Molly held up an immense calendar with highlighted dates of December twenty-sixth through January third and the clowns gave each person a handout.

Tess joined in the enthusiastic applause and was pleased when the clowns came running back in, ostensibly for "curtain calls" but actually so that, wigs in their hands and now speaking, they could answer questions and go into more detail concerning the plans.

Tess had heard that a construction detail was being sent but was amazed by the work already done. Hank Jameson, an older member who owned the local lumberyard, regretted he wasn't well enough to accompany them but volunteered to make available and pay all expenses for any size truck necessary to haul donated lumber, other materials, and sleeping bags.

In addition to giving an account of the plans about which they were being told, Tess saw that the handout had a tear-off portion inviting volunteers to participate. There was a list of ways they could make a commitment to help with the venture: going on the trip; providing funds toward expenses; supplying a van in case these could be used instead of renting a bus; buying materials; continuing in prayer for the hurricane victims and those helping to alleviate suffering; and ended with "Other Offerings."

Most parents with small children and some of the others left immediately after the skit, but most stayed to discuss what had taken place or to crowd around the clowns, asking questions.

Tess went to help a single mother get her two preschool youngsters—one sound asleep—to their car. Fastening the four year old in his car seat, she kissed him and said, "See you Sunday, Mickey, okay?" The drowsy child kissed her back and continued waving as long as he could see her.

She was welcomed back with a smile and half a wink by Pete, still in white face. Smiling back, she joined the outer ring of those around him.

Tess and Pete were among the last to leave. It took him some time to remove his makeup and change back into normal garb. Tess looked up at him as he carried the empty roaster to his car. "You did a great job! I had no idea you were into clowning."

"See what an exciting guy I am?" he teased, grinning crookedly. "Full of surprises."

She suspected this was true. "I can hardly wait to see what's next."

"I'm still a novice at clowning," he said modestly. "I

never thought of doing it until I went to a Sunday school conference last winter. Just for variety, I sat in on their clown workshop—and loved it."

"I can tell you do. And you're good at it."

"Pastor Jim thought he wasn't ready for it tonight." Pete laughed. "He really got into it, though. I believe he won't need much arm twisting to do it again."

"I wondered. I've never known him to do anything like that, so I was more surprised at him than you. After all, I don't know you very well."

He helped her into the car. "We'll have to do something about that."

But she decided he didn't mean it when she heard nothing from him for several days. *Why should I let that bother me?* she demanded of herself as she sat alone in church for the Thanksgiving Eve service. Still, she wondered why he was not there.

She spent all day Thursday with her father, who lived several miles away in the house where she had grown up. She didn't feel right in the big old place now that Mother was dead—or, more exactly, now that Dad was married to Jeannette, who was only nine years older than she.

Dinner was delicious and nicely served. Tess made a special effort to admire changes in the house but she missed the way things had always been. It must be difficult for a new wife brought into a house that had been made into a home by a deceased, beloved first wife.

She thought of her own apartment, which was comfortable and adequate. Although it had everything she needed and was a good place to come back to, she didn't think of it as "home."

When Tess invited them to her apartment for Christmas dinner, her father looked from her to Jeannette. "What do you think, Jeannie?"

The dark-haired, slender woman's hands clasped tightly in her lap. "Either there or here, Richard. Whichever you prefer."

He shook his head. "I need your honest opinion. It would be easier for you. . . ."

She hesitated. "You know I love cooking, so that's not the question. But I'll go along with what you want."

He rubbed his hand through luxuriant reddish brown hair just beginning to turn gray at the temples. "Well, I've had Christmas here for the past twenty-eight years, two years before you came along, Tess."

Tess could tell he would prefer that tradition. "And it would be nice to keep it that way," she finished for him.

His face wore an almost apologetic look of gratitude. "If you don't mind."

Partly to make him feel better, she said, "I'd have loved having you, but it will be simpler for me to come here this year. I wasn't sure if I'd even decorate a tree this season."

Her father leaned forward and she knew he was about to insist on being at her place if it made that much difference. She rushed an explanation, "A work group from church is leaving for the Miami area the day after Christmas to do construction or whatever's most needed by that time in cleaning up after Andrew. I'm planning to be with them if I can get clearance at work."

She was committed.

When did I decide to do that? she asked herself on the way home. *I've been thinking of it a lot since the clowns' presentation, but hadn't realized I'd come to a conclusion.* The subconscious was a marvelously complicated entity; she was pleased with its decision.

She went to the college the next day "for just long enough to work out that problem that came up Tuesday" and was amazed when she looked at the clock. She had spent over five hours in her vacation-emptied department. The rest of the long weekend, however, was hers, so she shopped for Christmas and met friends for lunch on Saturday—things she had not taken time for since the fall term began.

On Sunday afternoon she made stops at three different nursing homes to visit elderly people from church and deliver small potted poinsettias. Only during the late afternoon and evening did she get out books and notes to prepare for these last weeks before finals.

Frowning, she glanced at the clock as the phone rang. Nine-forty-nine. Who would be calling at this hour? "Hello?"

"Hi, Tess. Have a good Thanksgiving?"

It wasn't too late at all! "Hello, Pete." Perhaps she shouldn't show her pleasure after his not even contacting her since last Sunday, but. . . . "Yes, I spent it with my father— traditional turkey and all that."

"Me, too. Pumpkin custard, pecan pie—the works. I've returned at least several pounds heavier than when I left."

"You were in Connecticut for the holiday?"

"Yes. I thought I'd mentioned that. But with my not wanting to speak of the clowning till I did it, I probably missed other things, too. My brother and sister were home for the day with their families, so we had quite a time!"

"It sounds like fun. How many of you were there?"

"Let's see . . . five of Matt's, four of Lynne's, two grandparents, an uncle and aunt, and my parents. Seventeen of us. We had a great time."

Had he miscounted? Or did he have a guest with him? Maybe she'd rather not know. "How old are the children?"

They talked about the little ones, ranging in ages from nine months to seven years, and then he asked what she had done the rest of the long weekend. "At least I'm glad you got away from computers and studies for a little while," he approved.

Tess said she appreciated that but, since she had been foolish enough to take three subjects this semester, she would have to live with the consequences. Apparently he took that as a hint to let her get back to her books, for the conversation ended shortly thereafter.

She sighed as she replaced the phone on its cradle and reached for her lesson. She certainly had a lot to learn socially as well as scholastically!

Why hadn't she told him of her decision to go to Miami? Because he hadn't asked, that's why! She wanted him to want her to go with them—or at least be interested enough to ask. She sat there staring at the offending phone, then picked it up and dialed.

"Why, hello, Tess," the voice responded. "Is everything okay?"

She glanced toward the clock. "I'm sorry, Pastor Jim. I was studying and didn't realize it was after ten. Were you getting ready for bed?"

The minister laughed. "I'm ready—yes; going—no. In other words, I put on pajamas and a robe when I got back from a call, but I'm here in the recliner reading a book on spirituality and the church."

"Sounds deep."

"Actually, it's not as interesting or helpful as I'd expected. But I'm only on chapter three, so there's still hope."

"I won't keep you." She still felt apologetic, particularly since her reason for calling didn't bear close scrutiny. Just because she had been miffed at Pete's not asking about her decision was no reason for deliberately giving the news to someone else.

"I could have waited till tomorrow or Wednesday night—or next Sunday, for that matter."

"Don't worry about it, Tess. I'm not, that's for sure." His voice was reassuring. "I'm glad you called. Can I help you?"

"Sometimes I forget you're the preacher and are always getting calls for help," she said slowly. "This is something different. I've decided that if I can get vacation time I'll go with you to Florida."

"Great!" She couldn't doubt his enthusiastic approval. "I—we'll love having you!"

"There's still room?"

"Of course. If there weren't, we'd make room, even if it meant arranging for an extra van."

"Oh. . .well, thanks," she stammered. "I wanted to make sure at this end before notifying the school. . . ."

The next day she received that approval. She wondered many times as the weeks sped by if she had been out of her mind to say she would go. She could have used that class-free period to get caught up with things that had been put off much too long. Or she could have gone to bed early at night and treated herself to reading a novel.

One day, she hand-delivered to the head of the Social Studies Department a proposal she had been working on. Occasionally, the college gave credit for an Independent Studies project, so she asked Dr. Prentiss to consider her getting this if she did research and presented a major paper on volunteerism.

She would like to present a well-documented account of her group's trip and activities, along with various individuals' reasons for going, whether they had done anything like this before, what they got out of it, and whether they felt they would be willing to do it again.

Dr. Prentiss asked a number of questions that, having already been thoroughly considered, she answered to his satisfaction. He had to clear this with others in the department, so she didn't get the affirmative reply until the twenty-third.

In the meantime, she took finals in all three courses—and earned As in each.

Pete went home the weekend of December nineteenth for his family's holiday celebration. When he saw Tess on Thursday as they were leaving the seven o'clock Christmas Eve candlelight service he said, "Having off from school only this one day, I've been running around like crazy helping load the truck and finalizing trip plans."

"What about tomorrow?"

"Tomorrow?"

"I was wondering. . .are you celebrating Christmas with someone from the church—or something?" She felt herself blushing—maybe he had plans of a personal nature and would think her prying.

"Nope. Afraid not." Apparently seeing her dismay at his being alone on this most wonderful of holidays, he put his hand on her shoulder. His voice and face showed he was comforting her. "I'll be fine. . .I promise."

If only she were hostessing the noon meal at her apartment! It was too late for that now.

She waited until nine-forty-five before going to the phone. "Jeannette, are you planning for anyone else there tomorrow?" she asked after the usual greetings.

"No, it's just the three of us. Would you like to bring someone?"

She was making it so easy. "Do you know Peter

Macfarland, the man who's coordinating our trip to Florida?"

"Who he is—but we don't know him."

"Well, I was talking with him for a minute after the early service tonight.   As it turns out, he has no plans for tomorrow and I. . .well. . . ."

Jeannette's warm voice covered Tess's hesitancy. "We can't have him eating a solitary dinner in a restaurant or at home on Christmas Day," she stated. "Bring him with you—or have him meet you here, whichever's best for both of you."

Tess didn't tell her father's wife that either choice would be excellent as far as she was concerned. She would call back tonight if Pete would not be joining them.

She half expected difficulty in telling Pete she had made these arrangements but he accepted as soon as she quoted Jeannette's words of invitation. "What time shall I come for you?" he asked.

"Would eleven-thirty be okay? Dinner's an hour after that, but perhaps I could help with something. If she lets me."

"Problems?"

She hesitated.   "This is her first Christmas as my stepmother and. . .sometimes we're not sure what or how to say things to one another."

"That can lead to uncomfortable moments."

She agreed. "We're still overly conscious of 'working' at making things go well. The important thing is our both loving Dad and wanting him to be happy. And we don't choose to be rivals in any way."

His voice had a quality that seemed to come from some deep-seated well of understanding. "You'll make out great, Tess. And I'm looking forward to being with all of you tomorrow."

She had wrapped gifts for the other two last weekend but now tried to figure what to give Pete. It didn't seem right to have nothing for him when they opened presents tomorrow, but it was too late to go to a store. For that matter, she had no idea what to buy for him.

She returned for the second time to the tiny "guest room," where her computer and files took up much of the space not occupied by the spool bed and an antique dresser. Standing in front of the tall bookcase, she noticed the Contemporary English version of the New Testament, recently put out by the American Bible Society.

Drawing it from between two other versions, she opened it and thoughtfully turned pages. He would probably like this—if he hadn't already bought one for himself.

But that's true of any purchase I'd make for him. I've never been in his home. I really don't know much about him. Seeing him at church or in that restaurant hardly counts.

She remembered the leather Bible cover she had bought for her father the previous year. She had later decided not to give it to him when she realized that on the few occasions he came to church he didn't carry a Bible with him and when—or if—he used it at home, it wouldn't need protection.

Let's see, was it—yes, here it is on the closet's top shelf. In its original wrapper. She had been busy and waited so long before returning it to the store that she figured they probably wouldn't refund the purchase price.

Thank You, God, for making something this good of my neglectfulness, she prayed impulsively as the warmth of her expectations for the next day tinted her cheeks.

three

Christmas morning! There was a smile on Tess's lips even before she opened her eyes in the early dawn. She stretched, then relaxed again under the warm covers. A few snowflakes had been falling when she went to bed, but she could wait to find out if the ground was white.

It didn't smell like Christmas and she felt momentary regret. Perhaps she should have gone to cut a tree this year, though it didn't make sense when she would be leaving early tomorrow.

She rolled onto her other side. She had had no idea how much she would miss not going out to get a tree. According to pictures and stories, her parents had taken her every year since before she could walk. Even last year, when Dad was dating Jeannette, he and Tess drove to Rossiter's Cut-your-own Tree Farm on the Saturday after Thanksgiving and spent hours looking for just the right Douglas fir.

She pushed the covers back, got out of bed, and felt with her toes for her slippers. Going to the kitchen, she prepared her first tea of the day and a bowl of cereal. She put Christmas music on her stereo, to go with breakfast, and made a list of things still to be done before leaving for Florida.

She had remembered to stop the paper delivery. Mrs. Kirkpatrick, the elderly woman in the apartment next to hers, had agreed to collect her mail and to keep the three plants that Tess had taken to her yesterday. *Maybe that's why I so miss having a tree; there's nothing green and alive here.* But she didn't convince herself that that was the reason.

Returning to her bedroom, Tess counted out the under-garments, socks, and pajamas she would need. Many work clothes were piled on the guest bed but only a couple of skirts and dressy blouses.

Would there be opportunities for swimming? She doubted it, but got out her one-piece blue suit, just in case. Sleeping bag, soap and detergent, towels and washcloths, several pairs of athletic shoes, work gloves, rainwear. She would have to wait to pack her hair dryer, toothbrush, and other everyday items, but she noted these on her pad so she wouldn't forget them and have to buy replacements.

It was after ten when she called her mother's aunt in Florida. "Merry Christmas, Aunt Freddie," she greeted.

"My goodness, it's Theresa!" the delighted voice said. "I hope you're having a very good one, too, my dear."

"Yes, I am, thanks. A friend and I are going out to Dad's for dinner and I'm expecting to enjoy myself. But what about you? What are you doing today?"

She need not have worried about Frederica Bollway, she realized, when the eighty-six-year-old woman explained enthusiastically that six of "the girls" had already gone to a "simply wonderful" church service and were leaving in an hour for a restaurant nine miles away that advertised what looked like a "scrumptious Christmas buffet."

"You know how I love buffets, Theresa. Cooking for just myself, I stick mostly to meat, potatoes, and a vegetable, so when I go to a church dinner or buffet I try a little of all sorts of goodies."

Tess said she understood this feeling, then assured Aunt Freddie that all was well with her physically, emotionally, and job-wise.

When told of the trip beginning the next morning, Freddie insisted Tess must come visit. "It's less than two hours away, which is nothing compared with your two-day drive to Miami."

"I don't know what our schedule will be. I'll bring your number and call Monday or Tuesday."

"Make it before eleven in the morning or between nine and ten at night. That way I'm sure not to miss you."

Tess laughed. "What a social life you lead!"

"It's busy, anyway," she stated briskly. "Now you remember to call me—and plan to come for dinner. Bring a friend along, since that will make your drive more enjoyable."

Pete helped carry gifts to his car and didn't seem self-conscious about going for Christmas dinner at her father's home. He fit in comfortably with Dad and Jeannette, and Tess found this helped everyone.

Jeannette welcomed her assistance. Tess mashed potatoes and made gravy, while Dad carved the turkey. Pete transferred pickles and olives to a cut-glass container and carried the filled serving dishes to the dining room.

The conversation and banter were more natural than Tess could remember in these past ten months. "Thank you, Pete," she whispered in a moment they were alone, but she couldn't amplify that to satisfy the question in his eyes, as the other two came to the table and sat down.

Dad gave the prayer of blessing and Tess's lips moved with the familiar words she had heard since an infant. She had often wished he would pray thoughts of his own, and yet today the continuity, the sameness, warmed and satisfied her. She silently added her own prayer to his.

The meal and the afternoon were most enjoyable. Only after she was alone in her apartment that evening did she dwell on certain aspects of it.

For the first time, she regarded Jeannette as a friend. Although there had been twinges of pain when she first saw Dad with other women, she was pleased that he had overcome his intense grief enough to go out socially. He took several to dinner and for evenings out, but had assured his daughter that, since he knew he could never find another wife like Susan, he was seeking only companionship.

Well, Jeannette certainly was nothing like her mother, but Tess could, as of now, thank God for her father's choice. These two, both widowed after years of loving relationships with fine spouses, had been hurting and lonely. But now, they were together, happy, and fulfilled.

Christmas music on her stereo accompanied the last tasks to be done before leaving in the morning. And then, with a kitchen towel over her lap, she cracked and ate walnuts while watching a Public Broadcasting special in which a fine British actor played Joseph. She had never thought much about what he went through as the husband of Mary, the one chosen by Jehovah God to be the mother of God's child.

He must have loved her very much.

Tess's right hand fumbled for the switch to turn off the alarm then came back under the covers. Four-fifteen, already. With leaves gone from the trees, a wan square of light coming from the street lamp shone on the wall to the right of her bed.

She started to roll over until the realization struck her—this was the day she was heading for Florida!

Quickly getting out from under the covers, she straightened them and pulled up the colorful handmade quilt she used as a bedspread. She padded to the kitchen and put her tea in the microwave to heat while she showered and shampooed.

By the time she got back, the tea was very strong but she thought she would need the extra caffeine. The toasted english muffin with peanut butter tasted really good. She dried her hair and got dressed, then packed all her clothes in either her garment bag or suitcase.

It was time for one last check. Yes, the electric stove

was turned off; everything was as it should be. Loaded down with her sleeping bag and luggage, Tess headed for her car, and nearly panicked! A man was coming up the walk toward her. The street light was behind him so all she knew was that he was a big, broad-shouldered man—striding purposefully.

Should she drop things and run? But then Pete's voice was saying, "Good morning, Tess. I forgot to ask yesterday afternoon if I could stop for you. And I was afraid you might have gone to bed early."

It was all she could do to keep from showing Pete how he had frightened her. "I...thank you," she said, willingly giving up the luggage he reached for. "It is best to not have all of our vehicles parked at the church while we're away."

He smiled as he placed her things in the back of the big closed truck he had parked by the curb. "Excited?"

"I really am, though I slept right up till the alarm rang."

"Me too. And that was real early. This Peterbilt was loaded on Thursday, but kept in the fenced lumberyard for safekeeping. I had to go there this morning to pick it up."

Tess climbed into the wide seat and fastened the seat belt on the right. "I wonder how many are at the church."

"On my way to pick up the truck, I saw Pastor Jim and others arriving."

"I would have gotten there on time," she said in a small voice.

"I know that, Tess." His hand paused in the act of pulling his door shut. "It's just. . .I wanted to come."

Both doors slammed at the same time. "Thanks."

Head cocked slightly, he looked at her for a moment before pulling away from the curb. He must have decided not to continue in that direction for he began telling her of calls he had had the night before from volunteers asking questions even that late. "I think a few are wishing they hadn't signed on for this."

"I suspect there are more of us who were unsure at first, then got convinced as today approached." She was rewarded with a beaming smile.

The last three of the twenty-one were late. While the rest waited, initial assignments to vans were made for those who "didn't care where they rode." For the first leg of the journey, Pastor Jim would go with Pete and anyone wishing to do so could trade-off with him or anyone else at the first stop.

In case they got separated, each vehicle was provided with a list of the truck and rest stops where they would be pulling off. Unless changes were announced later, they would wait for stragglers to catch up.

Takeoff was within ten minutes of their schedule and for Tess the miles passed quickly. They had nibble foods with them, but the three vans and the truck stopped at one-fifteen so everyone could get out and stretch. At that time they opened up the lunch that had been packed for them— sandwiches, fruit, cut vegetables, and cold drinks.

They already noticed a marked change in temperature and by the time they stopped for the night at the church in

South Carolina, nobody was wearing a winter jacket. Tess was glad she had worn layers, for her lined windbreaker had been shed shortly after lunch and now even her sweater was too warm.

Pete had called ahead from their last stop to give the approximate time of arrival, so the parishioners of First Baptist, where they were going to spend the night, would have enough time to prepare a very welcome baked ham dinner.

"There was nothing to it," the chairwoman of the food committee declared when the Pennsylvanians thanked them for their thoughtfulness and exclaimed over how well everything was handled.

"The butcher presliced the meat and tied it, so all I did was put it in the oven here, take it out, cut the cords, and arrange it on serving platters. The other women made their big pans of baked beans and macaroni and cheese and salads and cake at home and brought them in time for your coming."

It sounded so simple, but Tess had helped with too many church activities to believe there was "nothing to it." She was pleased when some from the host church stayed to share their song time and evening devotions.

They had brought some camping cots in the truck but decided to sleep, fully clothed, in their sleeping bags on the floor of the large conference room. A moveable wall was positioned to make separate areas for the men and women. When that was done, most were more than ready to call it a night. Only a few senior high and college students were still singing around the piano down the hall when Tess fell asleep.

She was one of the first ones up in the morning and, still wearing the sweat suit in which she had slept, she went to one of the separate men and women's three-stall bathrooms on each of the two floors. She was glad to be finished washing before the rush but wished she had gone earlier to heat water for tea and instant coffee.

Pastor Jim was already in the kitchen and greeted her with, "I beatcha, Tess! The hot water's in the pot on the stove and I just got back from Dori's Donut Shop down the street."

"Our pastor's got fantastic domestic as well as ministerial talents," she teased.

"This is about the extent of them," he demurred, waving his arm toward the things already mentioned.

She didn't argue with what she knew to be true: As a bachelor he did his own cooking, cleaned the parsonage, and took care of his laundry. She helped set out napkins and cups and fixed herself some tea that she carried back to the conference room. Most of the sleeping bags were empty; some were rolled up. "Come on, Natalie. Time to rise and shine, Krystal," she said briskly. "Hurry and get around, for we leave in," she glanced at her watch, "thirty-eight minutes."

Natalie, a high school senior, sat up, yawned, then grinned. "This is just like home," she said. "I'm always rushing in the morning." Picking up her towel, washcloth, and toiletry case she hurried from the room.

Long-haired, beautiful Krystal, however, rolled over with a groan and slid down farther into the quilted bag. Tess looked toward Molly who, at sixty-four, was the senior woman on the trip. Molly walked over to Krystal and said, "Might as well learn this at the beginning, Krystal. We go to bed at night in time to get whatever amount of sleep's needed in order to fit into the group's schedule. So get up and pack. We're now down to thirty-six minutes."

Krystal's face and attitude showed very well what she thought of this, but she pushed herself up and flounced off in the direction of the women's bathroom.

One of the other women raised her brows. "I was afraid we'd have trouble with her."

"Oh, I don't know," said another. "She was active in a lot of things in high school and she's in her second year at college. I don't think she can be too bad."

"The trouble is, Krystal's always managed one way or another to get her own way...to not have to fit in with what others want. I told the pastor we'd have trouble."

Tess was about to respond but Molly beat her to it with a calm, "Let's not borrow trouble, okay? Let's assume she's just overly tired this morning and go on from there."

Doughnuts and hot beverages tided them over until midmorning, when most ordered Pete's suggested "hearty, working man's breakfast" of ham or sausage, eggs, biscuits, fried potatoes, and choice of orange or tomato juice. Krystal was an exception, preferring a sweet roll and soda.

Tess was riding in the same van with her during the

afternoon and made no verbal response as the young woman complained at the decision of the entourage leaders to keep going. Tess asked if anyone wanted "nibbles" from the bag beside her. Krystal and others emptied several boxes begun in the morning and also ate most of the remaining grapes.

By late afternoon, Tess began wondering if Hurricane Andrew had been as bad as reported. It seemed as though some signs should be apparent by now.

Before the end of the next half-hour, however, there was no doubt that a bad storm had struck. As they neared Miami's outskirts, Tess was horrified at the devastation on all sides.

Everyone was pointing and exclaiming. "Look there— at that tree trunk with a washer wrapped around it."

"See that trailer smashed right through the other one?"

"Those cars and trucks—they're almost welded together!"

Entire blocks consisted of nothing but rubble. An elderly couple with drooped shoulders stood holding hands, staring at a convoluted mess that had probably been their home. Small children climbed over what appeared to have been a large trailer that teenage boys were now scavenging.

Krystal said nothing. Tess, sitting beside her for the end of the trip, looked toward her and saw anguish on the lovely face. Unnoticed tears were running down her cheeks.

Without thinking, Tess put her arm around Krystal's

shoulders and the younger woman's agonized eyes turned toward her. "I. . .had no idea! No idea at all." The last word was almost a wail and Tess drew her close, relating acutely with the almost-silent sobs.

Tess shared a look with Pastor Jim who was presently in the front passenger seat as "navigator." His lips tightened before slowly turning upward at the corners. His nod was almost imperceptible, but enough that she was sure it indicated approval.

Of what he approved she wasn't positive—whether of Krystal's response to seeing the destruction surrounding them or of her helping Krystal. Her response was a slow smile.

The sights caused so much trauma that nobody else seemed aware of her and Krystal. Tess spoke quietly to the younger woman of the needs which they had only heard of before and of the work they had come to do.

They were grateful for instructions sent by the church in Dade County, where they would be staying. Even four months after Andrew, state and AAA maps were almost useless at some points because of detours.

They arrived with little difficulty but questioned whether they were at the right address until a small welcoming committee came to greet them.

From the street, the building looked little better than much of the area through which they had just driven. With its roof almost completely gone, the sanctuary reminded Tess of an after-the-bomb movie set.

Mammoth fallen beams had made kindling of the pews

and organ. Stonework and masonry had collapsed, leaving irregular portions of walls, devoid of window glass or, for the most part, of frames.

The voices of the new arrivals were hushed with shock and sorrow as they walked around to the reroofed and repaired Christian Education building where they would be given shelter from now, Sunday, until early the next Saturday morning.

Krystal, subdued, quietly carried in her own things and came back to help the others. Settling in took little time for, again, bed making consisted of rolling out sleeping bags.

"At least we have a roof over our heads," Molly said. Tess laughed and decided she was going to enjoy being with this woman.

As quickly as they could get their hands washed, they were seated at the long tables in the social room where food prepared by Red Cross and other volunteers was being served. The meal was simple but adequate and to Tess was much better than looking for a restaurant after the tiring drive.

People of the host church told them not to worry about changing clothes or if they would be a little late getting to the evening service that was being held in what had originally been the gym. Everyone understood that they had just arrived and they were grateful for the time and talent they were giving and were only too happy to have them.

Most of the choruses and hymns were familiar, and the

evangelistic message by Dr. Dunne was effectively presented. Tess appreciated his enthusiastic style of delivery. His delightful sense of humor manifested itself in anecdotes, apt descriptions, and twists of phrases.

Almost exhausted by the trip and afraid she would be too sleepy to get anything from the service, she surprised herself by being sufficiently invigorated to volunteer for table tennis before joining a group around the Social Room piano.

After that, she went to one of the rooms the women were assigned to sleep in and she went to bed. Everyone there was sleeping in their clothes on spread-out sleeping bags. But, during the night, Tess must have become chilled enough that she pulled up the flannel sheet she had brought in case she needed a light cover.

In the morning, Tess went to the women's restroom to clean up. Getting all of the shampoo out of her hair was nearly impossible in one of the small wash basins, but she managed to finish her morning ablutions before the big rush. She hung her damp bath towel on a line strung across the room and helped stack the rolled sleeping bags with hers in a corner.

She put on her oldest, most comfortable jeans and a long-sleeved cotton blouse so she wouldn't sunburn on her first day. However, in case she would be assigned to indoor work, she also carried a sleeveless top. She was grateful she had brought several pairs of work gloves—Molly had forgotten hers and Tess discovered after breakfast that Krystal hadn't thought to bring any either. It sounded as though they were going to need them.

four

Most of them walked the three blocks to their assigned work site. Pete brought the truck from where it had been stored overnight and Tess saw for the first time the many four-by-eight sheets of heavyweight plywood, long sections of spouting and guttering, bundles of shingles, and long rolls of the black, extra-heavy, waterproof material that she heard one of the men call roofing felt.

Their first job was a beatup rectangular building with tattered large plastic sheets covering the area where shingles and even some planks had been blown away. A mother and six children came out, introducing themselves as the Beaufant family.

Mrs. Beaufant welcomed them with big smiles and said how pleased—how honored—she felt that these fine Christians had come to help them. Somebody offered regrets that the house had been so damaged by the hurricane but she stood there, head high. "We're sorta lucky, though. None of us was hurt or killed...and we still have a home. Lots of folks here sure wish they was us."

Under the supervision of Hank Sorrison, a contractor from their home church, the men climbed up the provided ladders, checking to see how many of the remaining shingles were in good enough condition to leave. It had been established previously that, since the damage involved less than one-fourth of the total roof, it would be repaired, not replaced.

The other group of men, with Molly, Krystal, and one other woman, were soon on the roof of the house next door. They removed its torn plastic, which did little good after four months. With flat-tined potato forks and roof shovels they began ripping off all the shingles needing to be replaced.

The Ehrharts, who lived here, admitted that things got wet in their house when it rained, but they preferred staying here to moving into a tent city.

Mary Sue, as Mrs. Ehrhart insisted they call her, told them, "If we'd gone, bands of looters and worse would have destroyed what little we had left, and I wasn't about to let that happen. My kids need a place to call home."

At first Tess thought nobody could possibly live in the house on the next block where she and the rest of the women and an older man were about to clean up. One end of the roof was barely there but the exterior walls appeared intact.

Tess sighed as she stood near the curb, gloved hands on her hips, shaking her head. "It's hard to know where to even begin!" Then, squaring her shoulders, she moved into the yard and began to carry or drag fractured pieces of wood, metal, plastic, cardboard, and tree branches to pile along the street.

When they stopped for a break in midmorning, Matt Loomis commented, "At least people can see we've been here!"

Tess nodded. The front yard still didn't look too presentable with its weeds and gouges, but it was a debris-free island in these surroundings. It took the rest of the morning to partially clear the back yard. They finished that after lunch, before working on the inside of what had, until August, probably been quite comfortable living quarters.

Anything that could be used had been moved into the two crowded rooms still covered by a fairly good roof. They lugged rubble fallen from the ceiling, interior walls, and roof along with smashed, waterlogged furniture and beds. Tess was dismayed when she began wheezing, undoubtedly from the mildew and molds growing on the pillows and throw rugs she was carrying. Even the broken chairs, tables, and dilapidated chests of drawers were damp and discolored.

She used her inhaler and took her asthma medicine then put on one of the mouth/nose masks she always carried though hadn't needed for years. She kept on working in spite of the severely restricted breathing that was sapping her strength and energy. She wasn't sure how much longer she could continue.

At first her coworkers weren't aware of what was happening to Tess. When they did realize, they tried unsuccessfully to get her to return to the church. Molly, Pastor Jim, and Pete were especially concerned when they saw her condition at the evening meal.

"I'm sorry. . .," she began, but was interrupted by another spell of violent coughing. "I took shots for years. . .to desensitize me against. . .mold and mildew and haven't. . .had this bad an attack. . .for a long time. But then, I haven't been. . .handling the stuff like today. Perhaps wearing the mask. . .all day tomorrow. . . ." She was embarrassed at her wheezing and the necessity of stopping every few words to gasp for air.

"Come on, Tess!"

Pete sounded angry or provoked and she flinched. "I know it seems. . .irresponsible, but I didn't. . .consider the possibility of. . .breathing problems after. . .all this time."

"I didn't mean you shouldn't have come," he protested, placing a hand on her arm. "It's just that, if you insist on working, from now on you'll be on a different team."

"I'm not good. . .with ladders and heights." She could have cried, from frustration and disappointment as much as from feeling so bad physically. "I'd at least hoped. . .to spend my time in Florida. . .lugging trash and debris."

Pastor Jim's smile from across the table was meant to be encouraging, but there seemed a sadness there. "We'll see. The important thing now is for you to get over this attack."

It was while trying to finish her dessert that she overheard two of the roofers commenting about the Florida rulings being much more stringent than those in Pennsylvania. For one thing, here the plywood must be thicker—five-eighths of an inch—and that made handling the big sheets more difficult.

The thirty-pound-weight asphalt/felt roofing paper (which could be fifteen-pound back home) was bulkier to handle and must be fastened down with nails, not staples. This in itself would make things more difficult, but even worse was the stipulation that these nails must have special rings or discs between the nailhead and roof. "I could go twice as fast if I could just pick up a nail, pound it in, and keep repeating that."

The other roofer agreed. "I can't believe how time consuming it is to drive each nail through a disc before using it! I haven't built up any kind of rhythm at all."

"Where are these. . .nails and discs?" Tess asked.

Puzzled, they said they had been put in the room opposite the pastor's study. She asked them to go there with her. When they returned, the men were lugging boxes of nails and discs, while she carried several empty containers.

A group of eight went to play table tennis and the rest visited, while Tess tried pushing or pounding nails through the two-inch-diameter discs. She made little progress. *Dear God, please don't let me be a burden*, she prayed. *Help me feel good enough to keep going. . .to stop wheezing.*

Some time later, when Pete came to where she was sitting at the edge of the group, she looked up at him. "Did you win?"

He smiled wryly. "I never did excel at ping-pong and was worse than usual tonight." He took hold of her hand as it reached for another nail. "The important question is, how are you?"

"Fine."

He caught her other hand and silently held both of them until her eyes were raised to his. "That's not an answer, Tess. Let's try again: How are you feeling?"

She wanted to look away, but his brown eyes did not release hers. With dismay, she realized hers were misting. "I feel. . .better than during the afternoon."

Why didn't he say something? She tried unsuccessfully to control her wheezing. "All right, I don't. . .feel good. It takes so much. . .energy to breathe I. . .have little left for anything else."

He lifted the boxes from her lap and the chair beside her and sat down. "You don't have to keep working when you feel rotten, Tess. If you'll notice," his right hand arced to indicate those in front of them, "nobody else is, even though we're well."

"But I feel. . .so useless." She was stopped by violent coughing. "I came all the way down here. . .and wanted to be an addition. . .to the group."

"You are, Tess."

She coughed again and his arm came around her shoulders, pulling her close for a moment. "Do you hurt—physically?"

"Not. . .too much."

"Tell me about it."

She struggled to draw a deep breath and was afraid he would hear or feel its passage. "It's mostly the tightness. . .and wheezing and coughing. . .that bothers me. And my muscles are sore."

"Your chest muscles?"

"And across my back. . .and shoulders. And. . .I'm so tired." She had seldom felt so spent, so exhausted.

He moved one of the low-backed wooden chairs in front of her. "Lean your forearms on that and rest your head on them. I'll massage your back and shoulders and see if that helps."

She tried doing that but straightened almost immediately, shaking her head. "It's too difficult to. . .breathe when I lean over."

His fingertips gently touched her cheek. "That was stupid of me." He stood up and gently turned her so she was sitting sideways on her chair. "Let's try it this way."

His hands were warm and strong, yet gentle, as he massaged her shoulders, up her neck, and then across her upper back. She shivered and he stopped immediately, his voice solicitous. "Did I hurt you?"

Her left hand covered his where it rested for a moment on her shoulder. She shook her head. "It helps. . .it feels good," she admitted to him as he continued his ministrations.

He did most of the desultory talking—speaking of Thanksgiving and Christmas, of his growing up, and of their trip here.

Her voice was small as she finally said, "I feel guilty. . .keeping you here with me."

"Are you keeping me?"

His voice sounded relaxed and lazy. She whispered, "You're not. . .with the others."

His hand patted the top of her head, as she might do to

a child. "You worry too much, Theresa Kenneman. If I didn't want to be here, I wouldn't be."

She hesitated before asking, "Even if you thought. . .it would help me?"

He squeezed both upper arms and tilted her backward until she felt herself resting against him. "Even knowing you as little as I do, I'm aware you wouldn't ask for help. If I find something on my own to make you feel better, I claim that right."

"Oh." She would have loved to stay leaning against him but forced herself to sit upright again. He said nothing and the silence grew long. She didn't know quite how she began to speak of her mother and how close they had been. "She was young in her. . .outlook on life and enjoyed. . .all sorts of activities.

"I was thinking recently of. . .Christmas seasons when she went. . .as advisor on youth trips to. . .New York City for a day of. . .wandering and going to. . .the famous Christmas show."

"Um-hmmm. I—" She thought he was about to bring the conversation to himself, but after the briefest of pauses he said, "I'm sure you enjoyed them."

"And going shopping together. Though I usually . . .don't enjoy that. . .but with her it was fun."

The silence lengthened again before he said, "You miss her very much."

"Yes." She nodded, blessedly aware of his strength, his gentleness. "But I think. . .I know I'm adjusting better now. It was for the best, you know. Her death from cancer. . .was agonizing."

"I'm sorry, Tess."

She felt a touch on her bowed head and knew it had to be that he had leaned over so his head had rested there for a moment, for his hands didn't leave her back. She had not cried about her mother's death for a long time, but might very well do so any minute.

She slowly turned on her chair and felt his hand slide up to her shoulder again, so that his left wrist was against her neck. "Thank you, Pete," was all she said. She hoped he would realize it was for more than the back massage for which she was grateful.

Yet it was better that he not know everything for which she was thanking him.

Those who had been playing table tennis came over to tease Pete about quitting after losing three times in a row. "What a poor sport you turned out to be," Terry, one of the students, accused.

"It takes great wisdom to know the right time to move on," Pete intoned with mock solemnity.

To which the young man responded, "Or cowardice."

Pete sauntered over to where cans of sodas were being handed out. Reaching for two Cokes and a handful of pretzels, he challenged, "We'll find out who's the better worker when we start putting roofing paper on our house tomorrow, Terry. You'll have to go some to beat me there."

As he handed Tess her drink and some of the salty snacks, she murmured, "Couldn't resist that, could you?"

His eyes crinkled at the corners. "It was deliberate, of course. Terry's got a lot of leadership qualities and does a good job when he wants to. However, he goofs off a lot, and the younger kids follow his lead."

Pastor Jim, Molly, and Hank Sorenson came also. Hank, seeing how difficult it was to get nails through discs, disappeared for a short time. He returned with two-by-fours fastened just far enough apart that she could center a disc over the space and pound the nail through.

Molly got hammers for herself and Hank and the three worked together for the next half-hour. Pastor Jim brought empty gallon jugs from the kitchen and cut off the tops, leaving handles attached to bottoms. The prepared nails were dumped into these carriers, ready to be taken to the roofs.

Tess had difficulty getting to sleep. As she hadn't expected to need a pillow, Molly insisted on her own polyester-filled one being used to elevate Tess's head and perhaps make breathing easier. She also gathered the women to pray for her.

In the morning, Tess felt more like herself although she was bone-tired from the effort to get her breath and from lack of sleep. The horrible wheezing had let up appreciably, but her chest still felt as though confined by leather lacings.

She insisted on being told which place was next on the list for clearing a yard, and plugged away at dragging brush, roofing and siding fragments, and portions of furniture too damaged for use even by those who had lost everything.

She was almost too exhausted to continue when she saw the gloved hand beside hers on the end of a four-by-four beam and heard the worried voice saying, "You don't have to manhandle these heavy things, Tess."

She was sweaty and filthy, but so was he—and Pete had never looked better to her. "I am ready for a break," she said, but that was as far as she would let herself go in admitting her need for rest—and also the need to prove to herself that she could pull her own weight.

He must have realized how nearly spent she was, for Pete's arm remained around her as they walked the long block back to where he had been working. People were resting in the shade of the faded green, cement block house with its small gable over the front door. Some were seated, leaning back against it, while others sprawled on stomachs or backs.

The first strip of builder's felt had been applied along the lower edge of the roof so Tess asked, "Who won the workmanship challenge, Terry?"

"Technically, he did." The lanky, young, dark-haired man rolled over, crossed his legs, and put clasped hands behind his head. "But he cheated."

She looked at Pete with feigned horror, then back at Terry. "Pete cheated?"

"I wasn't keeping an eye on him, so at first I didn't realize he was going so fast because he was usin' those nails you fixed for him last night."

She was overjoyed. "It does work then—putting the discs on the nails ahead of time?"

Pete nodded. "Sure does!"

"Fantastic. Then that's what I'll do for a while before going back to that yard."

She drank cold water, ate salted crackers, and visited. When the others returned to the roof, she continued sitting in the shade with her back against the western side of the house.

As her hands worked, her mind wandered. Had any more crises arisen in the computer department? Were the secretaries continuing to make inroads on the backlog that must be changed or were they just keeping up with current work?

She felt herself tensing and was conscious of the increased huskiness of her cough. She emphatically reprimanded herself. *Let it go, Tess! You're here, where you got permission to be. And where you want to be. Stop worrying about your absence from work. Somebody will take care of problems if—as they arise.*

It was enjoyable to hear the banter and comments coming from the men and women above her. She wished she could feel secure on ladders or heights for she would love to be with the others, doing physical work directly involved with these restorations.

Oh, well. It wasn't as though she weren't helping.

As they ate lunch, Tess looked around the big tables.

"Where's Pastor Jim?"

Molly set down her glass. "It was shortly before you came for break that one of the coordinators stopped by. A volunteer from Tennessee who was doing canvassing got called back home, so they asked if we had someone to fill in."

"To 'canvass?' "

"To find out where groups like ours should be assigned. As I understand it, Pastor Jim will go from house to house and talk with people. He'll find out if they have insurance or are underinsured, how much damage was done, and what people like us can do."

"Oh." Tess hadn't considered how this was accomplished. "There are more aspects to volunteering than meet the eye."

Molly nodded. "And I wouldn't have missed this for anything."

Krystal, who had been silently eating beside her, murmured, "Me, too," and Tess smiled at her.

While washing her hands in the women's restroom near the church office, Tess asked the stranger next to her, "Are you putting roofs on also?"

A wry expression crossed the face of the frazzled woman who was probably in her upper sixties. "I wish I were."

Tess reached for a paper towel. "Why? What are you doing?"

"I almost feel like I'm here under false pretenses." The short, plump woman smiled slightly as she, too, dried her hands. "I am a volunteer, but not in the sense you are. I'm Carrie Jane, a member of this church and since the hurricane have been trying to help out as temporary secretary. But I'm having such awful problems!"

"Problems with people?" Was the influx of volunteers straining things too badly for the church?

"Not people. Equipment—or use of equipment. And computer software. Everything!"

"I can relate to that!" Tess exclaimed. "I'm something of a troubleshooter for the computer department at a college in Pennsylvania and—"

"You are?" The troubled face lit up with hope. "Could I ask a huge favor? Would you please come over to the office and see if you can 'troubleshoot' my mess?"

Tess looked from her to Molly, then back. "That's the least I can do considering all your church is doing for us."

Molly said to take her time—which was good, since Tess wasn't finished even by five-forty-five when Pete sauntered into the office, hands in the pockets of his relaxed-cut jeans.

Tess looked at him, then her watch. Pushing several computer keys to close down the system, she started to rise. "We've been so busy here we lost track of time."

She introduced Pete, and Carrie Jane declared, "This woman is the answer to my prayers!"

Pete's brows raised as he nodded. "I'm sure she is." Tucking her hand through his arm, he led her to the doorway as the women confirmed they would meet here again at eight o'clock tomorrow morning.

Tess wasn't sure how to react to his recent statement, but didn't have to when he asked, "What kind of difficulty have you got here?"

She looked sideways at him. "You'll never believe it, but it's the same sort of thing I've been dealing with back home. I suspect the secretary—the real one, not Carrie Jane—didn't have help or training when this first computer of theirs was purchased. Apparently, she taught herself a few basic things and did what she could day by day.

"She may have been able to call up a few files she wanted or needed but she must have done time- and nerve-draining searches for almost everything. There was no order nor organization, just hundreds and hundreds of entries."

"How frustrating for her successor!"

"It would have been easier if Carrie Jane were her 'successor,' for then she'd have felt she could call for professional help. As it is, she's filling in for what was expected to be a few weeks, but became months."

She wasn't completely over her asthma yet and had to cough. "The secretary lost everything with the hurricane, so was moved to the tent city. And now she and her husband are on an extended stay with a daughter in Kentucky, since his diabetes and blood pressure went way out of control."

"Those poor folks. And poor Carrie Jane!"

"She's been trying to work within the restrictions of this system—or lack of system. But she'd decided this morning to tell the church board they must get someone to take over immediately—that she couldn't stand it anymore!"

He hugged her hand against his body and beamed at her. "And then there was you."

She was warmed by his approval and touch. And yet. . . .

"But this isn't what I came to Miami for."

They walked several steps before he said thoughtfully, "It's not what we thought you were coming for, Tess. Apparently, God knew better."

Tess thought he looked very serious about this. "Taking that idea through logical reasoning, I might have to consider the possibility He wanted me to have asthma?"

He held up his right hand, palm toward her, a definite stop. "He often makes something good out of situations that appear all bad while we're going through them. I'll confess I'm never good at seeing what He's up to till after it's accomplished, but then I look back and realize, 'So that's what it's all about!' "

Several friends coming down the hallway after having finished their meal engaged in good-natured banter about her spending the afternoon in the church's air-conditioned comfort while they slaved on hot roofs. She tried to laugh, but it was Pete who told what she had been doing—and would be continuing with the next morning.

Pastor Jim's "final" cup of coffee was sitting on the table as they joined him. He was overflowing with stories about people he had talked with, what they had gone through, and their tremendous needs. The others were totally engrossed, not even asking questions or making comments.

Tess was finishing her cake when she saw Pastor Jim thrust out his hand, his voice roughened by emotion. "Thanks, Pete. Had it not been for you, we wouldn't be here."

Pete's hand firmly clasped his. "You're the one who picked up the challenge and ran with it."

"It was both of you—and Molly, here," Tess said, reaching out to stop the woman passing by on her way to the empty tray area, "who got the whole church involved by giving that clown performance."

Molly slid her tray onto the table and sat down. "That reminds me. We brought our clown outfits in case we wanted to do something here."

There was an upward lift to the end of that sentence, making it a question. Her bright eyes looked from one man to the other and Pete nodded. "I was thinking about that this morning when I saw all those kids playing in the street and climbing through the wreckage."

"So what's wrong with right now?"

"Have compassion, Molly," he groaned, reaching toward her pitifully. "Some of us aren't as young as we used to be and may find it difficult to roof all day, then clown at night."

She swatted his quavering hand. "And some of us keep getting better as the years go by," she stated, reminding them of what they all knew, that she was over twice his age.

Tess loved his infectious grin as Pete asked, "So which

of our vast repertoire of three semiprepared productions do you recommend for this evening, Madame Director?"

five

Molly leaned across the table. "How about *David and Goliath*?"

"With just you three?" Tess asked.

"Nope—four," Pastor Jim corrected, pointing. "He—David; she—King Saul." Drawing himself up as tall as possible and beating his thrust-out chest in the manner of Tarzan, he announced in a deep bass, "Me—Goliath and," with a gleeful look in his eye, "you—Narrator. You give the background and stuff like that, then are David's father and brothers and Goliath's backup army or whomever you choose to be."

"Lucky me!"

"Just so you appreciate the honor bestowed upon you of working with this renowned troupe."

"I've never even tried this."

Molly laughed. "These are persuasive chaps, in case you hadn't noticed. They first talked me into doing that skit at church and now I'll be in full costume!"

Pete was on his feet, heading for the door. "I'll dash outside and tell the kids who are always around while we're working. They can spread the news that the Pennsylvania Players will do a clown presentation in front of the church in," he glanced at his watch, "fifty-two

70

minutes."

Tess looked at the pastor in disbelief. "You're sitting there with that Cheshire cat grin on your face and letting him go out there to advertise a nonexistent show. Have you no scruples?"

He pushed his chair away from the table and stood up. "Scruples, yes; desire to squelch that crazy character, no."

"But look—I wouldn't have to put on the paint and costume and stuff, would I?"

"Worried?" He laughed out loud and reached for her tray. "I don't think you'll need to. Not this time."

She called after him, "What are you talking about, 'this time?' There may never be another one."

Pastor Jim brought the paints and costumes to the junior high department about the time Pete arrived to announce that he had talked not only to kids but some parents and even those working in the kitchen.

Tess groaned as she entered the women's bathroom to see if she could help Molly. "Well, there goes my hope that few people will show up to witness what we're about to do!"

"Things will go fine," Molly assured.

"Maybe for you three, but I have only the foggiest idea of what I'm even supposed to be doing."

Molly took off her shirt and pants and pulled on the baggy one-piece costume. "You grew up in Sunday school and have known the story of David and Goliath ever since I taught it to you when you were in my class of three year olds."

Her gaze met Tess's in the mirror as she applied paint to her face. "One of the really great things in this life is that the truths of the Bible remain that. If you have doubts as to what to do or say, your best course of action is to read what's in the Bible."

"But. . . ."

"You may want to give a brief account of the background of the story—who was fighting, the situation back home at Jesse's, and the youngest brother left behind to care for the sheep. You could mention the father's being so worried he sent David to the battleground with food and drink for his brothers—and about what he saw and heard there."

"You make it sound so simple!"

"Most of the Bible is. It's what you do with it—what it has to do with you that's hard."

"I'm. . .scared," Tess confessed.

Again their eyes met in the mirror before Molly turned toward her, interrupting the painting of a large, matching, dark blue, upside-down eyebrow. "I can relate to that. But I can assure you that you'll do a great job. I've seen you conduct youth, young people, and adult meetings and services."

"I. . .want this to be helpful."

Molly's fingertips were colored, which was probably why, as she reached up, it was the back of her hand that touched her young friend's cheek and jaw. "It will be. And you'll find you do have courage once you've begun.

"You love kids. I've seen it in your eyes and manner

when you're with them. And you want tonight to be special for them. Remember this from the fourth chapter of the First Epistle of John, Tess: 'Perfect love casteth out fear.' "

Those words kept repeating again and again as she returned to the room where the women slept.

Love. Yes, she did love these dirty little children in their devastated homes and community. . .and Molly. . .and Pete.

Pete? How could she say even to herself that she loved him? But. . .could she possibly say she didn't?

She was not going to dwell on this. No, she wasn't!

And yet the surprise, the shock of that thought made it come between her and the pages of her Bible. Let's see—First Samuel. . .about halfway. Ah, yes, chapter seventeen.

She went back and read Chapter Sixteen, also, toying with the possibility of putting into her narration Samuel's being sent by God to anoint David. But that wasn't part of this presentation.

She read chapter seventeen several times and from different translations, grateful she had brought with her the parallel-version Bible. She jotted notes of specific things she wanted to stress, in addition to the story's progression.

"How ya comin'?" Molly asked from the doorway, a construction paper gold crown topping her mop-wigged head.

"Okay, I think. And you look fantastic!"

Molly laughed. "King Saul was jealous enough of David to try pinning him to the wall. What would he do to me for making him look like this?"

The men arrived, Pete carrying something long and bulky in a bag. They had time for only a brief rundown of the order in which events would take place, for they wanted Tess outside to greet people as they arrived.

How could I have let them talk me into this idiocy? she asked herself as she went alone to the area that had been the front yard of the church. *Dear Lord, please don't let me start wheezing and coughing again.*

The street and floodlights were still pale in the twilight, but things seemed to stand out with unusual clarity. Massive cut stones still nestled against remnants of walls and the stumps marked where once-proud giants had shaded congregating worshipers. Something magnificent was gone, perhaps never to be restored to its previous grandeur.

But coming from different directions were individuals, parents and children, and other groups. Had any of these people attended, worshiped, in this house? If so, had they ever before arrived barefooted and in clothing less than clean. . .less than whole?

She crossed the courtyard to meet them, to shake hands, to hug the children. She was glad—elated—they had come. . .were still coming.

Molly had been right. She was not afraid.

Glancing at her watch, Tess realized it was time to begin. She had planned to welcome these people, but she found it more appropriate to do otherwise.

"My friends, we thank you for letting us come to your city for this week and to work beside you. We want you to know we admire your courage, strength, and faith that have brought you not only through the hurricane, but through these four difficult months.

"In speaking with the children," she smiled at them, "we mentioned our doing sketches or playlets while dressed as clowns. Being good hosts, they invited us to do one for you. You can thank or blame them for this evening."

The older people laughed and some of the little ones shifted self-consciously, while others looked proud. She invited them closer before introducing the "Pennsylvania Players:" Saul, the king of Israel (Molly arrived, her crowned head high, walking in stately pomposity); David, the shepherd boy (Pete swung boyishly around the corner of the building, barefooted and clothed in burlap); and then Goliath, the Philistine giant.

When Pastor Jim appeared, she laughed so hard that she was grateful she didn't have to speak immediately. He was walking heavily on three-foot stilts, wearing a hugely padded set of "mail" and other protective armor, and roaring angrily as he glared at Saul and David.

She sobered enough to begin. "This is a true story—one that happened long ago in a place called Israel or The Holy Land. The Lord God had given the Israelites this land years before, but the people already living there didn't want this, so war after war took place.

"At the time of our story, King Saul"—Molly bowed

regally, holding her crown on with one hand—"was the ruler of the Israelites. The Philistines, who lived between them and the Big Sea, the Mediterranean, were strong and powerful. And they had a secret weapon by the name of Goliath." Pastor Jim raised one hand and gave a curt little nod.

From then on, they acted out what she was saying.

"Goliath was huge, over nine feet tall—higher than ceilings in most houses," she said to help little ones get an idea of his size. "Goliath had been in major fights before and, big as he was, probably always won. Anyway, he or their army leader got what was considered a fantastic idea.

"One day when the armies were squared off from one another across the Elah Valley, Goliath came stalking out in front of the Philistines. In addition to his size, what he was wearing overwhelmed the Israelites. He had on a bronze helmet and leggings and a two-hundred-pound coat of mail. He had a massive javelin strapped to his back and in his hand was a heavy sword.

"His voice thundered, 'Do you need a whole army to decide this? I represent the Philistines. You pick your champion and we'll settle this in hand-to-hand combat! If your man kills me, my people will be your slaves. But if I kill him, then you become our slaves! I defy your armies! Send out your man to fight!'

"When King Saul and his army heard this, they were terrified. Nobody was big or strong enough to fight Goliath. Not even King Saul, head and shoulders taller than any of his soldiers, could possibly win.

"No Israelite volunteered, so that night and the next morning and each night and morning from then on the fearsome giant came into the valley, bellowing."

The children's eyes were bright with excitement, their eyes on Goliath, waiting to see what he might do.

"In the meantime, Jesse, the father of three of King Saul's soldiers, was worrying about his sons and how the war was going. They didn't have newspapers in those days, or radios, or TVs, so he sent his youngest son, David, to take food to his brothers and the captain of the army and to find out what was happening.

"After making the twenty-five- or thirty-mile trip, David arrived as Goliath came out to give his challenge again. David was horrified when the Israelite army turned and ran. 'What's going on?' he asked. 'Who is this heathen Philistine who defies the army of the Living God?'"

Tess now had to directly answer David's (Pete's) mimed question to her. "The giant has been hurling defiance and insults at us for forty days. King Saul's so upset that he's offered to the man who kills Goliath not only a stupendous amount of money but also marriage to one of his own daughters, a princess. In addition, this man's family will never again have to pay taxes."

"David" moved away from her, toward some of the audience and Tess continued, "Word got back to King Saul about David's talking to others about this situation. Now, he already knew David, who had been spending part of his time in the palace playing harp music for the king. Saul sent for the young man, who assured him, 'Don't worry, King Saul. I'll kill the giant for you.'

"The king was flabbergasted! 'There's no way a shepherd kid like you can kill that monster, who's been a fighting man all his life!' "

Tess could see the littlest boy in the front row sizing up David. Would he really try to kill Goliath?

"David explained that as a shepherd he'd clubbed to death wild animals that took lambs from his father's flock. 'God saved me from the claws and teeth of the bears and lions,' he insisted. 'He'll surely save me from this heathen Philistine who's making a mockery of Jehovah's troops.'

"The king was impressed by the bravery and words of this youth. So, since there were no other volunteers, he finally consented to David's being their representative and prayed that the Lord would be with him.

"In order to give as much protection as possible, Saul put on David his own specially made bronze helmet and royal armor. But when David strapped on his sword and tried to walk, he said, 'I can hardly move in this heavy armor!' And he removed it."

Tess wasn't sure that anyone was listening to her words now. Their attention was riveted on David struggling to lift and remove his invisible armor.

"Goliath was still out there heckling the Israelite troops, calling them cowards and shouting things he was going to do to them. He was infuriated when he saw David walking toward him, wearing nothing but his regular old shepherd boy's clothing and carrying only his shepherd's staff and sling.

" 'How dare you send a little red-cheeked boy out to fight against me?' he thundered. 'Do you consider me a dog, that you come at me with a stick?' And he started cursing David by all of his pagan gods.

"David had by this time gotten to the stream in the valley, so he stooped to pick up five smooth stones. He didn't appear afraid as he walked toward the ferocious giant, who was swinging his mammoth sword and threatening loudly enough for all to hear. 'You keep coming toward me and I'll cut you into pieces for wild animals and birds to eat.'

"David called back, 'You know how to fight with the sword and spear, but I have Jehovah, the God of the armies of Israel, whom you have defied. Today, the Lord will conquer you. He'll make it possible for me to kill you and cut off your head—and the bodies of your troops will be eaten by the birds and wild animals. All the world will hear of this and know that Jehovah is the God of Israel. And all the Israelites here will know that God doesn't count on weapons to work out His plans, nor is He impressed by human might. He will give you and all your men into our hands.'

"The Philistine lumbered toward him and as David ran forward he fitted a stone into the center of the leather strip. With a quick twirl of the sling, the stone was released and thudded into that small space between the giant's helmet and eyes. With a crash of armor and weapons, Goliath pitched forward onto his face, unconscious."

Tess paused, worried about the condition of her young

pastor whose hand had gone up to cover where the pretend stone had "hit" him. He didn't seem to have had much way of breaking his fall from off the stilts and now just lay there on the ground, motionless.

But the story must go on. "David had no weapon of his own so, grabbing the huge sword of his enemy, he killed the giant! The Israelites, cheering and yelling their battle cries at the top of their lungs, chased after the retreating Philistines, killing and capturing them.

"And they all knew, as David had predicted, that God is in control of everything."

Tess was pleased that the children in front of her were cheering also. But then she looked again toward Pastor Jim, lying "dead" upon the ground, at Pete, foot on his "conquered foe," and at Molly, crown askew but proud. She wished desperately that they had made arrangements for one of them to take over with a tie-in of their story with the situation in Miami.

But they hadn't!

Well, she would have to do something. "Even today, when things look dark and we wonder why bad things or disasters happen or how we can cope with what comes, the important thing to remember is that God really does care for us.

"He loves us and is with us, even through the bad times. It may not be so obvious as His helping a shepherd boy kill a giant, but when a friend lends a helping hand, when another prays with you, when you have the opportunity to help someone else—God is there.

"Jesus said that a person giving a drink of water to another in His name is giving to Christ. You have given your smiles and welcome to us, you have come to hear and see our clown performance and have patiently and courteously cheered us on.

"We thank you very much for showing us Jesus living in you. And yes, He lives in us, as well. If any of you would like to talk to us about this, or about clowning, or about anything else, please stay and visit."

It was late when they got to bed. At least twenty of the "audience" had remained, talking and visiting. A young man and woman went over to sit on a fallen pillar to talk about some spiritual matter with Pastor Jim, still in white face though without stilts and armor.

Tess took some of the teens in Molly's van to bring back pizzas and they all ate and had an enjoyable time together. It was Molly who finally brought things to a close by stating that if they were to work hard the next day, they needed to get to bed.

Tess didn't sink into sleep immediately, even as physically exhausted as she was. She kept thinking of the work she was doing in the office, of the skit they had done tonight—and that she had not called Aunt Freddie! She had waited too long in the morning, so had planned to do it after the evening meal. She must be sure to call after breakfast.

And she must also get back to making more notes on her

laptop computer. She had done some on her way down and her first night here, but she had felt so rotten yesterday and this morning that she had neglected this.

These resolves made, her mind returned to this marvelous evening. What fun it was to be with this group—especially the three who did the clowning. How was it that she had not come to know Molly as the terrific woman she was? Memories of her as an "old" woman teaching a Sunday school class must have still remained in Tess's mind all these years, keeping her from appreciating her as one of the "youngest" sixty-something adults she had ever known.

And Pastor Jim. She had respected and liked him, but it was mostly as "pastor," not as friend, a man only five or six years older than herself. She thought back over this evening, at him thumping his chest and growling, "Me—Goliath." And his taking that crashing fall when "killed" by David's stone. And his counseling with that couple.

She rolled over, willing herself to go to sleep, yet finding this not so easy to accomplish as to dictate. There was Pete also to think about—not that he was the least in her consideration. Had her mind deliberately left him until last so it could dwell on his attractive person?

She smiled in the darkness, glad nobody could know of her thoughts. He was so funny. So kind. So caring. It was he who had come for her at the office—and helped when her asthma was so bad. It was he who had massaged her back and shoulders and neck.

She could almost feel his strong, capable hands doing

this and hear his concerned voice telling her not to push herself, but to relax and get better.

And yet, even though his arm had been around her shoulders then, even though he had held her hand snug against his body as they walked back from where she had been working, even though their gaze frequently met laughingly or warmly or with friendship, he had made no effort to be more than just a friend.

Well, that's what she wanted, wasn't it? Her plans had been laid out precisely: She was going to put everything she had into doing her work and taking all the college courses she could manage toward getting her degree. She was not going to get "involved" with anyone as long as she was doing this.

Her twisted smile this time was at her own expense. It looked like Pete was "helping" her in this way also—helping her keep that resolve.

One part of her tried to keep from wishing this were not so.

Tess glanced up at the movement in the doorway and saw him there. Pete's voice and manner were brusque and demanding, though his smile belied this. "Hurry up, woman. It's lunch time!"

"I know. But I told Carrie Jane I'd keep going here till noon."

"It's after that." He pointed toward the big clock with its hands at twelve and two.

"And then I kept thinking of one more thing to do," she finished, closing down the computer.

Carrie Jane jumped in to justify her. "You have no idea how much she's helped me! Not only has she straightened out the files so I can find things, but she's put in programs for record keeping, and business letters, and the church newsletter, and memos, and all sorts of wonderful things!"

He put his hand on the older woman's shoulder and gave a friendly squeeze. "I was teasing, Carrie Jane. Honest. I know she's talented and generous and always gives her best."

They didn't touch as they walked to the cafeteria area. Her thoughts of the night before ruled out her casually takin his arm and his approving comments to Carrie Jane, while making her feel great, also made her self-conscious.

In a way she wished he would direct this sort of thing toward her—of course it was best he didn't.

She was reading too much into too little! He thought of her as a friend, nothing more.

They carried their filled trays to where Molly sat at the end of a noisy group and their conversation moved through discussions of the previous night's activities to the roofing this morning.

Tess remembered to tell them, "This morning I called my elderly aunt who lives over on Florida's Gulf side and up a ways. She absolutely insists I visit there tonight. Might I borrow your van, Molly?"

"Of course. You know that."

Tess smiled appreciation. "Frederica Bollway is my

mother's eighty-six-year-old aunt, the last of her genera-
tion and one feisty lady! I do want to see her while I'm
here."

Pete asked, "How far away is this?"

"She said it would take about two hours, so I'll leave
early, about four if that's okay."

He groused to Molly. "Ya just can't get good help
nowadays! She sits in that air-conditioned office all
morning and leaves at four to go visitin'!"

Molly slapped his arm affectionately (as Tess would
have liked to do). "Stop picking on the girl. Her work's
every bit as important as ours—probably more so if the
truth's known. I just wish I knew something about
computers."

Tess was about to offer to teach her but Pete announced,
"I'll ride along with you, Tess. You might be glad of even
my company when you're making the two-hour drive
back."

She felt warm and suspected she was blushing like a
schoolgirl. "That's not necessary."

He frowned at her. "I didn't think it was, Tess. However, you don't know these roads any better than I do, so
perhaps a pilot and a navigator are called for. Will your
aunt object to an extra person?"

"She'll be glad for it. She suggested I bring a friend with
me, but I didn't want to take anyone away."

He picked up his sandwich in both hands, saying, "Since
you're 'taking me away' from my work, I'd better eat fast
and get back up on the roof. I wouldn't want people

thinking I'm not doing what I'm being paid for."

He bit off a huge mouthful and started chewing rapidly. Knowing she was being teased again because of her overdeveloped sense of responsibility, she rolled her eyes. "You're incorrigible, Peter Macfarland."

He grinned as much as possible with his cheeks bulging with food. He reminded her of a playful chipmunk, but it was better not to say that.

six

Tess walked out with Molly and Pete and was delighted to see that their group had finished several roofs as far as possible. The state requirement that their work must be approved by an inspector after decking, flashing, roofing paper, and drip edges were installed meant that another team coming later would have to put on the shingles.

In the meantime, these homes were protected from rain. Those living in them could now begin to use all their space instead of crowding into the driest rooms.

A number of children and some adults came up to Tess, talking about last night's program. She was puzzled that they spoke to her rather than Pete until she realized that she was the only one they recognized. She introduced Pete as "David," and called up to Molly, already on the roof of a small house, to have her wave to her "admirers."

Fearing another bout with asthma, several tried to discourage her from going with them to clear away debris from another yard. She assured them she would be okay if she stayed outside, and was especially glad she had done so when she found she had helpers. Children, still off from school for Christmas vacation and probably bored, were eager to assist.

They wanted to know about Pennsylvania, about snow and sledding, and asked if people really did go out with parents to cut down Christmas trees. A few days earlier she had been sorry she hadn't done that this year, but now reveled in her memories, sharing with her young friends traditions that were taken for granted as a child.

She didn't stop for a break and found when Pete descended from his roof to walk to the church with her that he hadn't, either. They got cleaned up and were on their way northwest shortly after four.

"It's amazing," she said half an hour later, "how quickly we go from devastation to relative normalcy. Few of these homes seem to have been damaged."

"If so, it wasn't bad, anyway." He seemed completely relaxed driving and made comments about things they saw.

"It's nice to have things growing at this time of year."

"But I'd miss the change of seasons. We always did a lot of hiking and skiing and other outdoor activities, so saw nature in all her wardrobes. I loved each of them."

She would have liked knowing who "we" referred to, family or friends. But should it be some special friend, a woman, perhaps it was just as well not to know.

She spoke of Aunt Freddie. "She used to live in Duvall," the town just south of Fairhills. "When she retired, she was honored for having taught in that school district for forty-six years!"

"Forty-six?" His amazement was genuine.

"Sounds like forever, doesn't it? She went to normal school the summer after getting her high school diploma and began teaching in a rural one-room, eight-grade building that same fall. From then on, she took college courses each summer and often during the year, as well. Even after getting both her bachelor's and master's degrees, she kept on with continuing education and other courses right up till retirement."

"When you described her as 'feisty,' I thought maybe she was quarrelsome or difficult."

"Not Aunt Freddie. Oh, she was ready to fight for any student and for what she believes in, but she's more than willing to listen to the other side and try to work things out."

He shifted position behind the wheel and glanced in her direction. "Family traits?"

She was startled. "I would be. . .honored if people thought me at all like my Aunt Freddie!"

She was waiting for them, perky and spry as always. Tess didn't get to see her often since she had bought this two-bedroom, "low upkeep" house and moved south, five years before.

"It's about time you came to visit," Aunt Freddie stated while showing them around.

"You know I've wanted to, but with work and school it was hard to arrange," Tess explained. "And it sounds like you're as busy as I."

Aunt Freddie beamed. "Isn't that wonderful?"

Tess usually didn't think of it that way, but agreed, "It's good to have a lot of friends and interests."

"And it keeps you young."

Pete agreed. "It's certainly done that for you."

She patted his hand. "That's one reason, in addition to my arthritis, for my being here. Many friends back home got into ruts and found it too easy to find reasons for not doing things during the winter. That's no excuse for slowing down here."

"We still miss your cheerful face and your input on things in our lives and church. But I'm glad you're involved and happy here."

On their way to dinner in her big old Lincoln Continental, Freddie stopped at the church to which she had transferred her membership. "If you were staying longer, I'd bring you to Bible study/prayer service tonight. As it is, you can at least see where I worship and study."

Her guests exclaimed over the beauty of the airy, light sanctuary and how well the Christian Education building had been planned. She pushed open the door to a smaller, cheerful room with a desk and two chairs by an open window. "This is where I meet with three different children several times a week. The youngest and oldest need help getting their reading skills up to their grade levels, while the other's having difficulty with math."

Pete asked, "What grades are they?"

"Three, five, and eight—and their getting to those levels without anyone caring enough to see they got help is a crime!"

"They have the ability?"

Her fists were planted on her hips. "Definitely! Darrin,

the eighth-grader whom I began working with this summer, has already climbed from second to about sixth-grade level. And, most importantly, he has learned to enjoy reading."

"What does he like? Sports? Cars? Space?"

"All of the above. But he loves science fiction. So your old aunt," she said to Tess, "who had read almost none of that genre, is regularly getting these from the library and reading them. Incidentally, there's a lot of trash out there, but I pass on those I feel will help his reading yet not hurt him in other ways."

"He really does read them?"

"I ask questions and he shows good comprehension and retention. I've begun sneaking in exciting historical fiction and biographies and science, too, and bring him my Smithsonian and National Geographic and even Biblical Archaeological Review. He's not reading every word of these, but does some."

"Many subscribers don't read every word, either, for that matter," he reminded.

She smiled. "A point well taken. What I'm thrilled about is his not just looking at the pictures. He reads at least enough to answer the questions they raise."

Their stop wasn't long at The Center, a large, low, white structure where Aunt Freddie regularly went to swim and to take lessons in oil painting. As it was less than a mile from her home, she usually walked there each morning. She was disappointed that only a few of her regularly present friends were there to meet her guests.

It was after eight when they got to The Seafood Palace for dinner and Tess was so hungry that every item on the menu looked delicious. She was glad that her large tossed salad with ranch dressing was brought quickly for that and her roll were nearly finished before her Shrimp Threesome was set before her.

Dinner conversation wandered through many topics, from ancient family stories to the political scene to what could not be out of their minds for long—Hurricane Andrew. Aunt Freddie was upset about Tess's asthma attack. "You got those so bad when you were little! You were on the prayer chain many times, especially when you ended up in the hospital."

"I remember all too well, which was a major reason for my resisting your efforts to take me to the emergency room, Pete. I almost always got put in the hospital when I went there." That had been such a terrible period for her that she usually tried to forget it.

"But my shots had helped so much and for so long that I didn't expect even all that mold and mildew to hurt me. Needless to say, I'm not about to take chances like that again." She put an end to that topic after saying how grateful she was for all the prayers in her behalf, which must explain how she had gotten over this attack as quickly as she had.

Pete talked as much as either of them and seemed to enjoy his evening. Tess's suppressed yawn while finishing the lime meringue pie had nothing to do with being bored and she tried to convince them she wasn't sleepy.

However, as they started back to Aunt Freddie's home a few minutes later, her aunt insisted they stay overnight. Tess could sleep in the guest room and, "It's no trouble to make the living room couch into a bed for Pete." They could get up and leave as early as they needed to.

A deciding factor was her saying there was always lots of hot water, so they could get their showers either tonight or in the morning. They had both missed being able to do this.

Tess rolled over and checked the time. Four-forty-three. If this were daylight-saving time it would be nearly six—none too early to start getting up so they would have time for a full day's work.

At least these clothes I'm getting back into were clean yesterday at four. She used some of her aunt's deodorant and mouthwash, but that would have to do until she returned to Miami. Her aunt didn't own a hair dryer, but Tess could manage without that.

Aunt Freddie was in her kitchen preparing fresh grapefruit juice and visiting with Pete, who was replacing the embroidered pillows onto what was again an empire sofa. "You're bright and beautiful in the morning, Tess," he complimented.

"And so are you," she assured him. And he was. It was true, as he reminded her, that he needed a shave, but this made him look even more masculine and rugged.

She set the table and visited with her aunt while he showered. Aunt Freddie set scrambled eggs and toast before them, saying they needed good breakfasts to keep up their energy.

She also assured them when leaving that they hadn't been."too much work" and that she had enjoyed every minute of their stay. "You come again if you can get away," she insisted.

"I doubt that we can," Tess explained after thanking her for the invitation. "We have to leave early Saturday."

"Well, maybe you could stay an extra day or so."

Pete suggested, "Perhaps on the next trip we make?"

Tess asked, "You're already thinking of the next time?"

His face lit with that sudden boyish grin. "You betcha!"

Aunt Freddie inquired, "And how soon might that be?"

"Perhaps over Easter—or, to be more politically correct, as public school systems now have to be, 'Spring Holiday.' "

That threatened to bring on a conversation about the government as it pertained to the educational system, but they managed to get away before long. As they drove back, they at first spoke mostly of things concerning their visit. During a companionable period of desultory comments Pete asked, "So what about staying?"

"What?"

"Everybody's planning to leave Saturday morning, spend the night in South Carolina, and arrive home Sunday evening. Do you suppose Pastor Jim might consider staying until very early Sunday, giving the three of us a chance to continue working all day Saturday? With three drivers, we could take the truck straight through."

She had mixed feelings about this. He seemed to take

for granted that she would want to stay with them. She decided she was more flattered at being included than annoyed. "Let's ask when we get back."

They had no opportunity for this until the evening meal, since he and the other man and woman conducting the survey were involved in another area and ate their fruit, sandwiches, and beverages there.

A man near them, still suffering from sunburn acquired on his first day of working on roofs, said, "You've sure got it made, Pastor Jim, out doing surveys while we're doing the work!"

Tess almost jumped in to defend the importance of what Pastor Jim was doing, but realized in time that some undoubtedly still figured she had taken the easy way when helping with the church computer. She was relieved at Pastor Jim's looking innocently toward the speaker. "Would you like to trade places with me tomorrow, Earl?"

"No way!"

"I can go over the information and forms with you tonight and you can go into those houses and ask questions."

"Hey man, there's no way I could do that."

Pastor Jim's eyes didn't release the other's. "Then I'd say we each have an individual niche to fill, wouldn't you, Earl?"

Pete broke the moment's silence by asking Pastor Jim about staying for the extra day. The young minister nodded. "An excellent idea. I'll get the opportunity to work on roofing that way."

Earl looked uncomfortable as he leaned forward over his plate and ate rapidly. Pete went on, "The truck's front seat is plenty wide for elbow room and you, Tess, and I can take turns driving and sleeping. It shouldn't be too hard going back to work Monday morning."

"If I recall correctly, that's what you did when you came down before—and that would have been much harder since you were starting with a new class in a new school system that day."

Molly stopped by their table to inquire, "Shall we do the 'Christmas' clowning tonight or tomorrow?"

The men thought it would be better on Friday and Molly reported she had asked Krystal to narrate this time. They gave Tess hints and suggestions—and the extra clown outfit for her role as one of the down and out strangers seeking the Meaning of Nativity. She was grateful to have longer to prepare mentally than the few minutes she had had two evenings before.

Later, while pounding roofing nails through tabs, she decided Pete had deliberately mentioned in front of everybody their staying for an extra night. He had just as openly spoken of their being with her aunt the night before. They had nothing to hide, but she wouldn't have deliberately given more material to possible gossip mongers. On the other hand, it would probably have been worse for people to wonder about where they were and what they had been doing.

The point of a nail jabbed her finger. It wasn't bleeding, so she continued her work.

Morning. A new day—the last workday here for most of the crew. After breakfast, she walked out with a group and admired again how much had been accomplished. She was still surprised at the variety of roofs on these one-storied houses, for most shown on TV had seemed to be simple, straight, front and back surfaces. The majority of these had hipped roofs or mini-gables over the front door or other places, thus requiring flashing in gullies and more cutting and fitting.

"Did you notice how slightly slanted these roofs are compared with those at home?" Molly asked Tess.

"With no ice and snow, that's probably more than adequate."

"So there's almost no chance of falling off."

Tess looked at her speculatively, fearing what would be coming—especially when Molly called to a worker already on the roof, "Is the surface dry, Earl?"

"Dry as bare rock at noonday."

Molly had her hand on Tess's arm, steering her toward the ladder leaning against the house. "You've got so much courage and strength in many ways, Tess. How about climbing up there to hammer in some nails?"

She couldn't help pulling back. "I. . .don't think I can."

"Let's try it, okay? Just hold on to the sides, put one foot on a rung and the other on the one above it. And keep climbing. That's all there is to it."

The idea was mind boggling. "I couldn't possibly swing around to get off the ladder and onto the roof like. . .like Earl did a minute ago. Even if I managed to climb up there."

"You can. I'll be right behind you and—Pete, you go on up and give her a hand," she commanded.

"Yes, ma'am," he said, snapping to attention, flattened right hand angled from his forehead, heels of his sneakers coming together silently.

He sprinted to the ladder and climbed up as agilely as a monkey. It looked so easy when others did this but it was Molly's encouragement from behind her and Pete's smile and outstretched hand from above that made her place a foot on the first, then second, and each additional rung.

She would not look down—she must not. She paid full attention to her handholds on the side rails. Her lips felt dry, hands slippery. Twice, she paused to wipe a palm on her jeans before reaching for another higher grip.

Her head felt funny. Eyes closed with weakness and then in prayer, she leaned her head forward against a rung. *Dear God, please give me courage to go on. I can't do this without assurance that You're with me.*

She felt a strong hand covering her right one and Pete's voice commended, "Good girl!" She looked up into the approving brown eyes and, unbelievably, was able to smile a little bit.

"Keep your hold on the ladder till your feet are almost to the line of the roof," he advised. "Good. Continue holding on as you reach out your right foot to rest on the roof...over just a bit." The outside edge of his shoe pushed against the inside of hers. "Now there's room for your left one, also."

He was not touching her now but his hands were near enough that she knew he could grab for her if anything went wrong. The roof felt substantial under her athletic shoe—and now under the other one.

She moved her left hand to the right side of the ladder and reached toward Pete with her right one. To her surprise, he shook his head. "You don't need me, Tess," he said softly. "You're doing everything just right."

It didn't feel "just right" to her, but if he said it was, she would take his word for it. She let go of the ladder.

Tess was on a roof! Walking on it! Maybe it was only a step or two, to make room for Molly who, right behind, came to give her a quick hug. Tess looked over her shoulder and saw Pete beaming like a proud father whose baby had taken her first steps. He declared, "You're quite a woman, Theresa Kenneman!"

"Come with me," Molly said briskly, starting up the roof's slant. "As you see, we've got the third strip of the heavy, thirty-pound builder's felt—this waterproof roofing paper—laid down across the roof. The first two were nailed every six inches at the edges and twelve inches otherwise.

"Here's a hammer and one of the nails you've been putting through aluminum tabs. Use them."

Tess stood there for a moment, feeling utterly incapable of taking the several steps to her friend. The tip of her tongue circled dry lips and she put up her hand to ease the heartbeat throbbing at her temples.

How would she get back down?

Well, she was going to have to, sooner or later. As it was, she was just standing here while the nine on the roof and goodness knew how many others on the ground saw her acting like a ninny!

She drew in a deep breath and held it as she took a faltering step forward. Another. She was near enough to where she was to drive in the nail that she could get down on her knees. Reaching for the hammer, she placed the tip of the nail she had been handed in what she hoped was the proper relationship with others. "Okay?" she asked Molly.

"Perfect."

Her first hit was tentative but the next blow drove it through the builder's paper and firmly into the wood beneath. She reached for several more from the cutoff jug into which the prepared nails had been placed for ease in handling. There was no longer hesitation on her part as she placed and pounded in rapid succession.

Pete gave a long, low whistle. "You've been hiding your talents, Tess!"

"I helped Dad build the garage. And finish off the basement. He's something of a perfectionist, so I learned early how to drive nails."

Molly sat down and motioned for Tess to do the same. "Occasionally, I have to stop what I'm doing and look around. Since there are no hills or mountains, this is as close as we get to a perspective on what happened here and what we're doing."

Tess sat beside her, hugging her knees. From here she

couldn't see down to the base of the ladder or even the yard of this house. The view of the street or beyond didn't give her vertigo, nor did the roof tops.

Pete was on his knees helping pound nails as Molly pointed out to Tess the six houses that had been repaired by their crew. They would be finishing this one soon. The one three houses over, the blue cement block one, should easily get done this afternoon.

The faded pink house over there across the street, where people were removing the last of the large, heavy, rectangular, cement tiles, had been begun only since they knew Pastor Jim and Pete would be working all day tomorrow.

Perhaps I'll be some help with that, also. If they do the work near the edges, she thought timidly.

Tess's arm arced broadly, indicating everything in front of her. "There's so much left to do."

"Yes. There is," Molly agreed. "Every one of those places with plastic covering its roof needs major repairs."

"Are people living in all of them?"

"I think so. At least that's the case with all we've worked on."

"It seemed that way. If we can call that living." Tess shuddered. "In the house where I was carrying all that stuff when I developed that attack, a family of four was crammed into one room. Oh, they could use the commode and the kitchen sink, but the roof's plastic covering had torn and their belongings in the rest of the house were destroyed."

Her head moved slowly to the right then left. "I never

saw people so. . .so overwhelmed by life. He had retired from a reasonably good job, their home and car were paid for and insured, and they thought they were okay.

"And, in one day, they lost almost everything. And then they found that their insurance company was one of those that went bankrupt because of Andrew. They had nowhere to go except to the tent city and figured, whether correctly or incorrectly, that they'd be no better off there."

She sighed. "Their lack of hope made me feel even worse than my wheezing and struggling to breathe. At least my suffering with that is now over."

Molly frowned at her. "You should have left as soon as you realized what was happening, Tess."

"I didn't expect it to get bad." She was silent for a moment before adding, "And yet there was a good side to even that. I keep remembering that, although they'd lived like that for four months, once they saw I was there to help and wasn't leaving with the first twinge of discomfort, the man came out to carry and drag some things, too."

"That's another example of the way God makes good come out of bad," Molly said matter-of-factly as she pushed herself up to her feet and reached to help Tess. "And now I'd better get to work before they fire me."

One of the men unrolling another strip of builder's paper heard her and pretended to scold. "And you wouldn't appreciate our docking your pay, would you, Molly?"

Tess would have liked to go back down the ladder right away—well, she wouldn't like to do that at all, but did wish she were already on the ground.

Pete had completed his hammering of the last nails securing the previous strip and got up to cross to the other side of the roof. His voice was light as he asked, "Ready to help with this one, Tess?"

"I'm not sure I'll ever be 'ready' for that, Pete," she confessed. "But I probably could manage more if that's a requirement for your helping me back onto the ladder."

He was instantly serious. "Look, Tess, I really don't mean to be demanding and nasty. It's just that it's important to deal with fears and hangups, even though that's difficult. And I do understand how you feel. I used to be terrified of snakes."

She shuddered. "I don't like them, either."

"Until one day I went to a herpetologist and talked to him about my fears and how this kept me from hiking except in winter. You can probably guess what he did— made me look at pictures of snakes and read about them and finally get so I could touch, then hold them."

She wasn't sure she could ever do that. "You're completely over that fear?"

He laughed ruefully. "Snakes are still not my favorite form of life. And they startle me if I come upon them unexpectedly. But I no longer have a debilitating fear and I do have a grudging admiration for them."

"So you're saying I don't have to camp out up here to prove I'm not scared to death, but in the meantime I can learn not to let this phobia immobilize me."

"That's about it. If you're positive you want to go down right now, I'll help you. Or," and there was that dancing

light in his eyes that often preceded a smile, "if you want
to stay up here and practice so you can be our third worker
tomorrow, I'll help with that, also."

From where she was standing near the center of this
shallowly sloping roof there appeared to be nothing more
dangerous than a hillside at home. She drew in a deep
breath before saying in a small voice, "I'll stay. For a
while." But she added a qualifier, "If you'll remain
between me and the edge of. . .disaster."

He reached toward her, his smile radiant. "Any time,
Tess! Any time."

seven

For a moment she thought he was about to hug her but instead he leaned over to pick up two hammers and he was all business as he showed her exactly what to do. She was high enough to see that the back of the roof was finished except for the drip edge being attached by men on stepladders.

She enjoyed doing this work that before she had only watched from the ground. She wouldn't let herself dwell on the thought of going down that ladder. But, when the job was completed, she found that with Molly at the bottom to "steady" it and with Pete talking her through the process, she could do it.

As her foot touched down, she heard spontaneous clapping and looked around at these friends whom she had come to care so much about during this week's time together. They were all smiling, and then she was, too. "I couldn't have done this without your patience and caring. Thank you."

A man called from the next roof for more of the "ringed" nails. Tess saw only a few dozen in the large can and asked, "Is this all of them?"

"Afraid so," Earl said. "Everyone was so busy trying to get our jobs finished...and I guess we thought these would be enough."

She looked toward Pete, hoping he wouldn't think her offer was an excuse for not going on to the next roof. "We'll need a lot tomorrow, too. I'll work on getting nails ready for then. . .and for the rest of today."

Matt Loomis joined her as she lined up aluminum circles along the narrow space between the two-by-fours. "How about my pounding nails in the center of each disc while you continue laying them out?" he offered.

"I'd appreciate that. And after a while we'll trade off so we get variety in our lives."

This went much faster and she enjoyed the easy conversation about things here, back home, and, especially, of the early history of their church. She knew he was always reelected as church historian at the annual business meetings and she had heard him speak at the church's one-hundred-fiftieth anniversary celebration eight years before.

She hadn't been much interested then, but was now fascinated by his story of the missionary who had come from Connecticut in the 1800s and traveled up and down the valley by foot, horseback, and boat.

Many residents liked and welcomed him, but he also made fierce enemies, among whom were the Doebly brothers. Along with several other drunken men, these two "tarred and feathered the preacher and rode him out of the village and a full five miles away tied him to a fence rail that had one end attached to a horse's saddle."

"Was he hurt?" Tess gasped.

"Sure was. The next morning friends found him in the woods, unconscious, still tied with leather thongs to that pole. They cared for and nursed him back to health and wanted to help him get another horse—his had been stolen or driven off—so he could return to New England.

"But he was a determined as well as dedicated Christian. As soon as he was well enough, he went right back to the same town and walked up to the older of the Doeblys. He stuck out his hand, palm up, and asked that they be friends.

"Jake Doebly was sober that early in the morning, but he still spit tobacco juice on the preacher's hand. That didn't stop Elisha Reichmann, however, for he said, 'That's all right, Mr. Doebly. I'll just keep on praying for you. The Lord God Almighty wants you for His own.' "

"That must have gotten a reaction!"

"Oh, it did. Jake threatened to kill the preacher then and there, but it didn't faze Elisha. He just said, 'In that case, I'll be in the presence of my Lord and God, so even for that I can be thankful.'

"Jake was so mad he drew his gun, but apparently there was something in the bravery—faith?—that got to him. Or, knowing that all the townspeople would be aware of it if he shot an unarmed man, he realized he'd better not do it. Whatever the reason, he turned and walked away.

"And the next summer at an open-air revival meeting, Jake Doebly was one of those who walked down the sawdust aisle and gave his life to Christ."

She had been so involved in what he was saying that she had paused in laying out discs, but she now did more before removing those that had been "filled." "That's a great story! And it will be even more wonderful if you tell me he was of the family for whom Doebly's Mills was named."

"It was for him, not his family, that that section of town was named. Once he got straightened out spiritually, the rest of his life changed, too. He'd worked in a grist mill as what we'd call a 'gofer,' I guess. He was a hard worker and advanced to more responsibility and finally bought the place and added to it and eventually became one of the most influential deacons in our church and the mayor of our town."

"Fantastic!" she exclaimed. "Do you know what I'm going to do? I'm asking Pastor Jim to have you tell that story in church as a children's sermon."

"Oh, I couldn't do that!"

"Of course you can."

"I'm no good at quoting Scripture and weaving in lessons and doing stuff like that."

She covered his strong, lined hand with her work-gloved one. "That has all the lessons and Bible woven into it, Matt. Any man with the strength of God, the love for His people, and the dedication that Elisha displayed would be an inspiration not only to children but to every single adult present."

He looked dismayed and she smiled. "Don't worry about it, Matt. God will give you courage, too. I know He will. It's just that...well, I grew up in our church and never even heard that account. Have you written it down?"

"Well, it's in my notes somewhere."

"Don't you see? Perhaps you're the only person in our congregation who knows about this. We can't have it lost when you're gone—which I hope will not be for a very long time," she hastened to add. "Please share these stories of the past that you've searched out and treasure."

Clearly, he was changing the subject when he called her attention to how nearly finished the group across the street was in removing cement tiles from "their" house. It would take some time for workers on the ground to gather and remove all the heavy, broken pieces of concrete sliding down that improvised ramp.

Several other women also helped drive nails through discs, so she was able to carry quite a lot to the house where Pete was securing yet another strip of builder's paper. He waited for her to come partway up the ladder before reaching for the cutoff jug. "Gonna stay and pound?"

She wanted—no, almost wanted to do this. "I'd better help with cleanup," she said. Forcing herself to look away from those warm, seeing-too-much brown eyes, she focused on the work being done on the pink house. "Do you think that will get finished tomorrow?"

He chuckled. "Depends on the help."

With raised brows she looked back at him. " 'Help' . . .like the people or like what they accomplish?"

"They go together."

"Like. . .perhaps I should get more practice?"

He tilted his head slightly and looked at her through narrowed eyes, as though this were a new thought he had to consider. "Since you mention it, yeah, I'd say that's not a bad idea."

Climbing the rest of the way wasn't nearly as bad this time, but she was extremely grateful for his giving a hand to assist her in getting from the top of the ladder to the almost flat roof. He asked, "Wanna look down this time?"

"No!"

She felt her face flushing from embarrassment at having been so emphatic, but she could think of nothing to add that wouldn't make her cowardice even more apparent. She was spared the need by his assurance. "It's okay, Tess. You're doing very well. I'm proud of you."

She looked down at the carefully nailed strips of builder's paper on which her feet were firmly planted. "You shouldn't be, but thank you."

On his way back to where he had been working, he dumped some nails into two other containers for those working on their sections of the roof. She waited for him to drop to his knees before she got down beside him and picked up a hammer.

At first she didn't talk much as she developed the rhythm that would accomplish the most efficient nailing. However, when he said they could review what they would do as clowns in a few hours, she was able to concentrate on that.

This time she had felt more confident, partly because she was better prepared. She had to admit to herself, though, that the main reason she had been able to lose her self behind the paint and inside the costume was that she was no longer Tess then, nor Theresa—she had become the wanderer.

It's strange, she thought while lying in her sleeping bag that night. *It's not that I don't like being me, but it's refreshing to be so entirely in the role of someone else that you even feel and think like that person.* She yawned sleepily. *Did professional performers feel like that?*

And then it was morning.

Everything was in turmoil. People finished packing their meager belongings, ate breakfast, and started getting into vans. When Molly hugged her and said she hoped the three of them would have a good trip coming back in the truck the next day, Tess found herself almost tearful and wishing she were leaving with this woman who had become such a good friend.

"Maybe I shouldn't be staying."

Molly drew back slightly. "Why not, for goodness sake?"

"Oh, I don't know. Maybe I won't be that much help."

"And?"

Tess confessed, "I guess. . .I was thinking that maybe it doesn't look good. . .my staying with the two men."

"Worried about your reputation?"

"Not really." She shook her head. "But with Pastor Jim being the pastor and Pete a teacher in the public school system. . .there's not going to be any stupid gossip or trouble for them, is there? If so, I could get my sleeping bag and other things and be back in a few minutes."

"Don't be ridiculous!" Molly said. "If you're up to driving straight through to Pennsylvania tomorrow after putting in a full workday here today, more power to you."

"We'll sleep some on the way. Spelling one another with driving, it shouldn't be too hard."

"You all have to be at work the next day."

Tess put her hand against the small of Molly's back and gently gave her a push. "Yes, Mommy. We'll be careful."

Pastor Jim, Pete, and Tess stood there waving until the last van turned the corner and was out of sight. Pastor Jim pulled his work gloves from his hip pocket. "Well, there goes our last excuse for not being on the roof."

"Race you to the ladder!" Tess challenged. Her long legs ate up the distance—but both men passed her as they crossed the final yard and took positions on either side of the goal, grinning in triumph.

She was panting from exertion, but laughing. "At least I tried."

Pastor Jim patted her back as though commiserating. "Had the distance been a bit shorter, you'd have won."

Pete sobered. "You did win, Tess. You won in being able to choose the ladder as your endpoint. . .and running like crazy to and not away from it."

"Oh." She could think of nothing more to say as she looked away, not wanting him to read in her eyes how grateful she was for his approval.

He hurried up the ladder and waited at the top to assist her as he had done before. Pastor Jim went to pick up the nails and hammers and by the time he joined them, they were unrolling the heavy roof covering.

Pastor Jim took her end from her and she wondered if this was his way of saying she didn't have to be at the very edge of the roof. Only after the unrolling was completed did he put in those nails that would securely hold the beginning of the strip and then worked across to where she had started pounding.

Pete took over the cutting and arranging at the other side of the roof and while he was doing this, she continued pounding nails. There wasn't much talking as they worked steadily at making the strip secure.

The process was repeated and when they stopped for a break they found Myron, the man of the house, wanting to visit. He had been at work the other days and they hadn't gotten to know him. "I didn't think our roof would get fixed by your group. Dottie, here," he indicated his middle-aged wife who was coming from the cement-block house with a pitcher of orange juice, "said everyone was leaving this morning."

They lounged in the shade of the house as the trees that had been in the yard had been reduced to splinter-topped stumps. Pete explained, "We're the only ones left and we'll start home very early tomorrow morning."

"How early?" Dottie asked, pouring juice into un-matched glasses.

"Five, five-thirty. . .somewhere around there."

They talked about Myron and Dottie's family, two sons and a daughter living "up north," and Dottie brought out pictures of their seven grandchildren. "What a handsome family you have!" Tess exclaimed, returning the snapshots.

"We think so." Dottie's round face creased with delight. "We just wish we could be with them more. They were all planning to spend Christmas with us this year—would be here right now if it weren't for Andrew."

Tess reached for her hand, recognizing the sadness that had overtaken her. "Now that your roof's fixed—or will be at least rainproofed by the time we leave—maybe they can come soon."

"I don't know. Much of what was inside—all the beds but one and the living and dining room furniture and most of the rest—is ruined."

"That does present problems," Tess agreed. She had not seen inside and only hoped these people hadn't left the mildew and rot as had been the case where she had developed that horrible difficulty with breathing.

Pete and Pastor Jim were at the ladder and Myron was carrying a hammer as he came from inside his house and followed Pete upward. Pastor Jim waited for Tess to precede him and Pete was there to help her should she need it. His presence gave her confidence to step out upon the roof.

They worked steadily for the next couple of hours, during which time two neighbor men joined them. It was noon when Dottie's dark face appeared over the roof's edge. "Ya'all hungry?"

Pete answered for all of them. "Starved, actually. I've

been trying to get these characters to quit long enough so we could go get sandwiches."

Dottie's smile was radiant. "We have a better idea. Instead of you going to get them, we're invitin' you to come eat with us."

Tess laid down her hammer, wiped her perspired face on her cotton sleeve, and stood up. "That sounds wonderful! I'm so thirsty I can hardly stand it." However, she waited at the ladder until the other woman got all the way down and Pete was beside her.

She desperately wanted his assistance—but he didn't offer it. Holding onto the ladder with both hands, she hesitantly planted first one then the other foot upon a rung. She carefully felt with her toes for the next lower one and started her descent.

Looking up as her feet touched the ground, she was rewarded by seeing Pete's right thumb and forefinger forming a circle while the other three fingers were extended. His lips formed silent congratulations: *You made it!*

She felt exhilarated—by having accomplished what she had never thought she could do and by his commendation. For a split second she felt sorry it was only during this last twenty-four hours that she had attempted to overcome her phobia. Her smile answering Pete's before he swung around and scampered down the ladder was one of pure joy.

Adding length to a picnic table and a card table was a long, narrow one created by putting on sawhorses the various two-by-four pairs of lumber they had used for pounding roofing nails through discs. The assortment of wooden and metal chairs had been brought from homes on which the Pennsylvanians had worked throughout the week.

Tess blinked to keep from crying as she saw the macaroni salad and baked beans, fried chicken and catfish, steaming cornbread, and even several pecan pies. "What a spread," she exclaimed, looking around at the twenty-five or thirty happy faces. "What a surprise!"

There was a lot of visiting and sharing of happy experiences as well as telling of how life had changed overnight for these new friends. "There have been many times," Effie Mae, a young woman with two small children, said, "when I just wanted to give up. It seemed like no matter how hard I tried, things weren't goin' to get better."

Dottie agreed. "We felt so hopeless. Nobody seemed to care, really care about our situation. Oh, we were given food and were permitted to go to a tent city or stay on in our homes. But there were so many needin' help that those of us who could 'make do' continued to do just that."

Pastor Jim's face showed compassion. "That was the main feeling of those we surveyed throughout Dade County. Actually, a lot of people and organizations are concerned but they, like you, are overwhelmed by needs."

Myron slathered butter on the large chunk of cornbread in his hand. "That's an important part of your comin' down here to fix roofs. You didn't have to take from vacation time to help us."

"And you didn't have to give those clown programs, either," Effie Mae stated. "But they helped, too."

This led to a discussion of clowning and of how they had gotten into it. The hosts could hardly believe it was here that both Tess and Krystal had had their first experiences with this ministry. They wondered aloud if perhaps they could start something like this in their churches.

Pete promised to send Myron a book about clowning that he had found helpful. He then stood up, saying that, since they had already consumed most of the pie, they had better get themselves back up on the roof.

Time and work went speedily, with even more neighbors helping up there and clearing away below. The sun was throwing long shadows by the time the final strip of builder's paper was nailed across the top and the drip edges were securely fastened. Someone on the roof gave a cheer and suddenly everyone was hugging and laughing.

"We made it! We really finished the job," Tess cried, her arms around Dottie, who had been working alongside her husband.

"Isn't it wonderful?" Tears of joy were running down Dottie's cheeks. "You'll never know how much we appreciate what you've done."

There was no sign of morning through the tall windows as Tess, alone in her assigned room in the Christian Education building, got out of her sleeping bag, fully clothed, and headed for the women's restroom. *It will be good to wake up tomorrow in my own apartment and take a hot shower and shampoo and get back into my regular routine,* she thought wistfully.

She looked at the tanned, oval face in the bathroom mirror and saw its smile. She would never regret coming here and working and meeting all these new people whom she had been able to help even for this limited amount of time. The experience had been so much different from what she had expected or even hoped for.

Bonuses were ticked off on the fingers of her left hand even as she washed with her other one. Getting to know the people of her church better—especially Pastor Jim and Molly and Pete—though not necessarily in that order. Sharing her computer expertise. Getting over her fear of ladders and heights, at least being able to function at a one-story level, anyway. Adventuring into clowning. Having that wonderful time with the people here yesterday.

And the developing relationship with Pete.

She should erase that word "relationship" even from her thoughts. But no! It was a perfectly good word, with an all-encompassing meaning of association or compatibility with another person, and should never have been trans-muted, cheapened into implying sexual activity!

She put on her last clean blouse and jeans and packed everything else as compactly as possible, but left out the windbreaker, which would probably be needed as they neared home.

Pete was waiting for her inside the exit door and reached for her luggage. He didn't say "Good morning" as he had done other times when she was looking lovely or wide awake or anything. He just grinned as he said, "You're gonna be surprised."

"What's up?"

With a sideways tilt of his head, he indicated the door and said, "You'll see!"

She preceded him to the cement-and-brick walk and was met by Dottie, who threw her arms around her. "We had to come again and wish ya'all a good trip home."

And then the others—nine of them including two children—were all speaking at once and thrusting candy and homemade cookies into their hands.

Myron was lugging a polystyrene foam container holding sodas, leftover fried chicken, and other things from the day before. Hefting it into the back of Pete's truck, he said in response to Pastor Jim's concern about returning the box, "Don't worry about it. Refrigerated materials come packed in these to the lab where I work. I'm always tryin' to give them away instead of throwin' them out."

eight

"I don't know," Tess said as they were able to get on their way only ten minutes later. "I never expected them to be so responsive. Maybe it was because there were just the three of us."

"Or perhaps because it's the weekend, and the ones who were were working all week are home yesterday and today," Pastor Jim suggested from his seat by the passenger window. "During the week when we were working as a crew we outnumbered them and they may have been intimidated."

Tess admitted, "You're right. I did talk to people— some. But I'm afraid I didn't try very hard until yesterday . . .except with children occasionally and after the clowning performances."

"None of us was really good at this." Pete sighed. "I didn't make any real effort to draw people out if I didn't get an immediate enthusiastic response." He glanced over at his passengers. "I'm glad God directed us to stay. At least there's a chance that our friends from yesterday realize we really do care about and for them."

She nodded. "We had a definite advantage there, because of our clowning. They seemed to appreciate that."

Pastor Jim agreed. "The part I'm especially pleased with is that the sociability was their idea. I asked them this morning if this sharing was a neighborhood custom, and they said that when they were working on the roof with us and helping us clean up was the first time some of them had even spoken to one another! Can you believe that?"

"Maybe this will continue now that it's begun," she said, hoping this would be the case.

"Even if it doesn't," Pete said, "what a great memory it will be for them. And for us."

Tess nodded. "My grandmother used to tell of wonderful times of spontaneous community kindness as she grew up on their farm. Like when the father of some kids showed up at their one-room school with a horse-drawn bobsled to take all of the kids and the teacher for a ride. And another time all the farmers went with their families on a late-fall Saturday and got the corn crop husked and put away for their neighbor who was ill."

"Now that's being good neighbors!"

"It is indeed!"

They spoke of individuals they had met in Florida—of Francis, the man still limping from injuries suffered during the hurricane, who had managed to work on the roof yesterday, and of a child who seemed fine now, although she had been in the hospital due to a skull fracture she had sustained at that time.

They also talked about the church that had hosted them and the Red Cross workers. Tess shifted into a more comfortable position. "I'd expected to get around more while we were there."

"I'm sorry about that," Pastor Jim said. "I saw quite a bit, since I was out talking with people. I should have asked if anyone wanted to take a van and drive around."

Pete put in, "Some of us went out late the second morning we were there. It was awful, even after four months."

He could have come to the church office and asked me to come along, Tess thought. It would have been nice to be asked—and to have gone. However, as rotten as I felt that day with my asthma and as busy as the secretary and I kept, I'd probably have begged off. Pete obviously didn't seem embarrassed when he mentioned this, however, he had not meant to hurt her feelings in leaving her behind.

They made a practice of frequently pulling off the highway to stretch and at least walk around the truck a few times. Pastor Jim took the second turn behind the wheel and it was when Tess finished her stint that they broke out the chicken and salad.

They ate quickly at a wooden picnic table and Tess still had Coke left when she climbed into the truck to fasten the center seat belt around herself.

It wasn't until late afternoon that talk became more centered on things at home. She suspected Pastor Jim's thoughts must have many times been on their church, just as hers had to be dragged back from worrying about things in the computer department.

She and Pastor Jim included Pete in their discussion of how to improve the senior high Sunday school class and get the students involved with activities. "I assumed this trip indicated they were active," Pete said. "Aren't the three who were with us leaders in the youth group?"

"I wish they were," Pastor Jim admitted. "They have lots of leadership potential, and use it in varying ways at school— sports, drama, music, what have you. All good things, mind you, just not church-related."

"Their parents?"

"Not too active themselves, nor inclined to push our activities. Of course it is hard to fit everything into busy schedules. . .and they're all good students."

They talked about the three, one of whom had been raised in the church while Terry and the other had come within the last three or four years. Pastor Jim pulled himself into a straighter position. "I'm encouraged that they all worked hard on this project and seemed to really enjoy doing it."

Pete said thoughtfully, "You mentioned a while back that you wanted us to tell about our trip at the beginning of next Sunday's service. You were planning to include the young people?"

"Of course."

"I was wondering. Could you perhaps have a separate session for them with their peers, like a pizza or spaghetti supper? I know they got some pictures as we all did."

"I didn't get as many as I expected." Tess had hoped to take a lot. "And I'm not sure mine will be too great."

"But you did the writing," Pastor Jim said. "How much did you get on your computer?"

She hadn't realized she had been so obvious about this. "Quite a bit." And then she talked about her intention to use the material for Independent Studies projects.

"I saw you talking to folks from other areas. Did they help?"

"Um-hmmm. Especially those working on different details, like those spending weeks cooking for groups like ours."

"That takes dedication!"

"It certainly does."

Pete asked, "Do you have a specific plan as to utilizing the information you've collected?"

"Not firm," she admitted. "Not yet. I've been doing a lot of thinking and will finish my first stage proposal to submit before the end of this week."

"Will you be using your pictures?"

"I'm. . .not sure. The head of the department wasn't enthusiastic about that. I suspect she saw it as my way of wanting to let pictures do the talking, instead of my words.

"Since she doesn't seem to want this, I checked with the journalism department just before Christmas to see if I can do an Independent Studies photojournalism project there. With this, I understand that successful publication of the article is a necessity for receiving a good grade."

Pete looked surprised. "They do that sort of thing there?"

"I know of people getting credit for similar things, but don't know all their circumstances. Actually, I'd enjoy either project even without college credit, so I've nothing to lose by trying."

"And probably a lot to gain," Pete agreed.

Pastor Jim offered, "If you could use my pictures or if I can help in any way, just ask."

"Thanks, Pastor Jim." It was so typical of him to offer. "I've seen some of your photography. I may very well come knocking on your door."

"I'll be waiting, Tess."

Pete said nothing, but she was certain he would also help if she asked.

Darkness seemed to come awfully early and she turned the headlights on before she ended her stint of driving. They pulled into a truck stop where the meals were large, flavorful, and nourishing. Pete relaxed against the back of his captain's chair. "I'd planned to have dessert, but don't have room. How about you?"

"I'd prefer stopping for something a little later on," she told him and Pastor Jim agreed.

Tess shivered as they crossed the lot. "Next time I leave the truck I'm wearing my jacket!"

There was a coziness, a feeling of peace, warmth, and rightness, as they rode through the darkness. There were longer lulls between conversations, but these were friendly, comfortable silences.

They ate dessert around ten and the men teased Tess about her large butter pecan ice cream cone that turned out to be huge. She still had much of it left when the men had finished their black coffee and pie, so she took it along to enjoy in the truck.

She napped briefly before her next turn to drive, and was asleep when Pastor Jim pulled up in front of her apartment. She looked around, surprised. "We're home already."

Pete laughed. "It's only 'already' for the one who slept away the past hundred miles."

He opened the door and got out, then helped her, which she appreciated as she was a bit stiff from being in one position for so long. Pastor Jim went to the back of the truck and they joined him there to retrieve her things. Pete insisted on delivering them, laying them on the Early American tapestry sofa in her apartment before heading for the door.

"Get a good night's sleep, Tess, and be rarin' to go come morning."

"You, too, Pete. I suspect you'll need it even more than I, with your postvacation third-graders waiting to greet you."

He didn't look tired as he smiled. "We'll both make it; I have confidence in us."

She closed and locked the door. Yes, he apparently did have a great amount of confidence in himself. And he inspired it in others.

She could still hardly believe she had climbed that ladder and not just once but several times. And she had actually worked on that roof!

Her morning shower was every bit as hot and refreshing as she had remembered. Maybe it was good that she had "done without" for a week if it made her more appreciative of everyday blessings. She stepped out onto the shaggy pink rug and dried herself with one of the soft, absorbent, pink towels that she then wrapped around herself. With a second large towel, she made a turban around her wet hair. Then she went to the kitchen to prepare tea and toast.

She had plenty of time to get ready, especially since she brought her tea and a sandwich of toast with peanut butter into the bedroom to eat. She breakfasted while dressing in slacks, shirt, and blazer.

Even bundled warmly, she shivered from the cold as she hurried to her car that started with no problems. There was light enough to see without headlights but the day seemed drab and colorless. The houses on her block were all white, not the pinks and blues and yellows of those that she had been helping repair.

Ah, but these houses had intact roofs, the shrubbery was well tended and manicured, and the bare tree branches still arched over the street. *How blessed I am, Lord. Please help me be more grateful. And help those poor people we met and the thousands of others who are in as bad or worse situations.*

She parked in her reserved slot, got out, and hurried toward the Bachman Administration Building, one of the oldest structures on the century-old campus. Its dark red bricks were well pointed and the pillars, window frames, and wide trim wore fresh white paint.

She went up the four steps to the wide porticoed area that graced many of the university's publicity shots, through the wood-and-glass door into a large entryway, and from there to the third door on the left, her office.

It's true she shared this with her secretary, but she had arrived early as usual and for the moment this was hers.

She hung her coat and hat on the brass rack and walked over to sit at her desk to shuffle through the stack of mail.

Envelopes that appeared to be Christmas-related were separated then slid into her purse for reading at home. Professional journals and advertising information were stacked on the far corner of her desk and next to them was a separate pile of business letters and memos that had to be taken care of immediately.

Oh, great! The permission to go ahead with the journalism project was in her hand! How much material did she have? She was certain there was enough for both endeavors. She transferred the high density microdisc from her pocket to her computer. As the printout was being done, she continued going through the pile of mail.

There was a special departmental meeting called for eleven-thirty today. And her secretary, Alicia, had left a note saying that the treasurer wanted her to call as soon as she got back. Apparently, there were additional questions concerning the endowment fund, about which Tess had notified people prior to her leaving.

She reached for the phone, back on the job and needing to touch base with everyone. She would be expected to give up-to-date information at the meeting concerning how things were progressing, even though she had been "on vacation" for a week.

The high-speed printout was completed before Alicia and some of those from other offices arrived. They wanted to know all about Tess's trip, and whether there really was as much damage as it appeared from what was shown on TV—or was this just "more media hype?"

She assured them things were worse than she had imagined—even four months after the hurricane. She couldn't go into detail, however, with so much work waiting to be done.

Alicia was unashamedly relieved by her return. "I was scared you'd have car trouble or something and I'd maybe have to fill in for you at the meeting!"

"Maybe I should have waited to come until this afternoon." She laughed shortly and glanced toward her desk. "I'll need all your input from this past week if I'm to get through."

The tone of the meeting was better than at any other time over the past two months. Christmas happiness? Probably not. There was usually more post-Christmas blues than euphoria in the dark month of January.

On her way home, Tess dropped off a roll of film and stopped to pick up the plants and week's mail from her neighbor. She was delighted to find that prints from film she had sent last Tuesday had already arrived. Sitting on Mrs. Kirkpatrick's couch, she shared these, telling of pertinent things that had happened and what she and her group had done.

"It's exciting, Tess, that you got to use your computer skills like that!" The loose-skinned, frail looking hands were clasped in the lap of the lavender plaid wool skirt and her blue eyes sparkled.

"At first I was disappointed that I'd gone all that way, only to be doing what I do at home. But it wasn't long till I realized this had to be of the Lord. There's no way I could have predicted getting my worst asthma attack in fifteen years on my very first day of work."

Then she confessed, "I felt sorry for me—and for my coworkers being stuck with me—and there He was, providing me with a job that nobody else was as well equipped to handle. And, by the time that was done, I was pretty much my old self again."

"Did you go to the hospital?"

"No—though Pastor Jim and everyone else thought I should."

"Why didn't you go?"

"Partly because I didn't want to be a bother." She rushed in more words as the other began to scold her. "I'd gone down there to work and was afraid that would end it. I've gone to emergency rooms before when this happened—and ended up being admitted."

"But—"

"I always carry my inhaler and other medicine with me, even though it's been a long time since I've needed them. With using these and staying away from molds and mildew for the next thirty-six hours—and having the prayers of my wonderful Christian friends—I got through."

"Thank God!"

"I do." Tess smiled as she got to her feet. Her neighbor

invited her to stay for soup and toasted cheese sandwiches but she begged off. She was tired and needed to get at least one load of laundry done. "I'm almost out of underclothes and every pair of jeans and the things I wore in Florida are filthy!"

Mrs. Kirkpatrick carried the two smaller plants as she walked with her to Tess's apartment, but left when Tess was called to the phone.

Tess slid out of her pumps and curled up on the end of the couch as she visited with Aunt Freddie. Yes, she had arrived safely in Pennsylvania. No, she had not had another attack during the rest of her stay. And they had, indeed, done clowning again.

Tess told of the wonder of their last day in Florida, with people coming to help complete that final roof and share food and spend time with them. "Of my entire experience there, that's got to be the highlight—except for our time with you, of course."

Aunt Freddie's hearty laugh hadn't changed with the years. "That was a good 'save,' my dear. But your visit truly was a highlight of this winter for me. And I want you to know that I like and admire your young man very much."

Tess would have liked saying that she did, also, but needed to keep things accurate. "He's not my young man, Aunt Freddie. Just a man whose friendship means a great deal to me." In response to questions, Tess reminded her about his coming to town at the beginning of the school term and about his sharing at the church supper concerning his earlier trip to Florida. "That's what inspired all of us to go and do likewise," she said. "And I do admire him."

Yes, things had apparently gone reasonably well at work while she was away. And her neighbor's care of the plants had been excellent, thank you. Her first pictures arrived today and others were being developed. Her folks were well, according to a phone call, but she wouldn't see them until the weekend.

As she replaced the phone she hoped she would see Pete then, too, if not before. He had been such a help in many ways.

He was not at the midweek service. He did not call. She told herself he was busy with school and—and what else? She saw him at church on Sunday. He smiled over the heads of people between them but didn't come to her.

Thinking back over their time together, she realized she knew little about his social life. Was he dating? If so, was he seriously—emotionally— involved elsewhere?

He certainly had not romanced her. If she had read too much into his kindnesses when she was suffering, that wasn't his fault.

But she wasn't willing to accept—not yet, at least—that her instincts were wrong. He had gone out of his way to show concern for her and he had chosen her to work with him in clowning. And to work beside him on that wonderful last day.

He was the one person who had reached out to her in that special way—to make her overcome or cope with her fear of heights. If he didn't care for her, would he have bothered? Would he have gone with her to her aunt's home so she wouldn't have to do all that driving by herself on unfamiliar roads?

She didn't know about these things. Or many other things about him.

But she knew a lot about herself. If he didn't call, if he didn't soon indicate some interest in her, she would not be able to keep from feeling hurt—perhaps devastated.

At work she had no time for fretting about this; there was always so much to do. She was good at her job and knew she could get everything she had onto the new system— if given enough time. The last major change, which had taken place before she came and primarily involved updating previous work, had been done over a three-year period. This was a complete change. What they expected timewise was unrealistic and she was missing some important documents and records, how many, she still didn't know.

Today was one of those increasingly frequent times when she admitted to herself she would like to resign.

She always thought and organized best at the computer, but now found herself taking over much of the dining room table for her projects for credit. She got permission at work to use their facilities to tap into library and other information services so she would not have to waste time tracking down sources.

She wrote letters, but primarily used phone calls to interview people who had done a lot of volunteer work. How she wished she could include in her two papers more of what she was learning!

Another week passed. One day after work she went to the mall and bought clown makeup, colorful wigs, rubber noses, and other things she thought might come in handy. She wondered if Pete had remembered to send Dottie the book on clowning. In case he had forgotten, she bought a paperback one and sent everything with a note to thank her and the others for their friendship.

Pete still didn't call, but Pastor Jim did—several times. As a result of his first call, she went to church early Wednesday evening and sat with him in the Family Activity Center, going over his pictures. She was awed by their quality. Love for the people was evident in the shots he had chosen to take.

She had considered her own pictures to be good, for they clearly showed the tremendous damage Hurricane Andrew had made and the reconstruction work accomplished by their teams and groups from other places. One of the shots she had considered almost professional in quality was of a house trailer's aluminum shell wrapped around what was left of a large tree.

Pastor Jim had taken a picture from almost the same spot. His showed an elderly man leaning on a wooden cane in his right hand while his left hand reached out to touch with all five fingers the scratched, twisted metal.

She whispered, "His home, the sorrow, the grief—it's

all there."

Pastor Jim's voice was solemn. "It was his daughter's home. His small grandson died there."

There were tears in her eyes. It was hard to even say, "How awful!"

His eyes remained focused on the picture in his hand. "The heartbreak—is everywhere."

"Oh, Pastor Jim." She wanted to comfort him as much as she wished she could ease the pain of the man in the picture.

The next one was of a little child. Tess had photographed boys searching through debris, scavenging, looking for treasures. The picture before her was a closeup of a barefoot little girl surrounded by ragged, splintery lumber and broken glass—and the child was crying.

"How did you get this?" she asked, hurting for the subject of this picture, too.

"I used the zoom lens. And I'm ashamed of having taken time to do that before I picked my way into that mess to carry her out. Her name's Betsy Ann and she's only three but was able to tell me how to find her mother."

The pictures continued. She finally looked up at him, her heart breaking. "How do you bear it?"

"Bear what?"

"Seeing the world like this. The pain, heartbreak, despair."

He riffled through the photographs and drew out several. "They're balanced by the love in the world, Tess. Things like this."

He held out a picture he had taken of her late in the afternoon when she was first helping the church secretary. "I look awful," she protested.

Pastor Jim would not let her pull it from his hand. "You felt so terrible, yet you wouldn't stop. And here you are," he said, showing her another, "that night when you were wheezing and exhausted, but pounding nails through discs. Because of your love and concern."

"Let me destroy these, please. I had no idea I looked that frightful."

"And you sounded that bad, too." His troubled gray eyes looked into hers. "I've seldom felt less helpful—more useless—in my life. I was upset you wouldn't go for help."

Her hand covered his. "You were a help. You and all who were praying for me."

"And you couldn't sleep."

"Not much. But," she took a deep breath and reached for more pictures, "that's enough about an incident that's over and done with. What's important is the other pictures you have here and the stories they tell. You've got to show these—get them published."

"They're not that good, Tess."

"They are. They really are."

She was sure his response of, "We'll see," was simply his way of terminating that discussion. He got up to greet the people coming for Bible study.

When he called the second time, it was to ask whether she would be going to the Association meeting, where people from twenty churches would assemble for their winter session. He had received an invitation for the Fairhills church to have a twenty-minute segment of the program to show pictures and tell briefly about its trip. "I'd appreciate your help, Tess."

"With what aspect of it?"

"To share what it meant to you to be with the group and to tell what you did."

"Comments of the other volunteers would be more typical."

"But that's why I need you. It's easy to get so wrapped up in 'purpose' that we lose flexibility. You did something different—and in a way only you could."

She hesitated. "I'll try, if you want me to, but I wish you'd rethink this. I promise not to be offended if you change your mind."

"I won't and you shouldn't, in that order," he said, voice warm with teasing or relief. "Let's get together with Molly and Pete and some of the others to choose slides and pictures on," the rustling of pages showed he was checking his appointment book, "Thursday night at...eight-fifteen, right after the Christian Education Board meeting?"

She glanced at the wall calendar, penciled in with things she must do. "Sounds okay. Good thinking to do it while you and I, at least, are already there."

She wondered if it would be awkward if Pete felt he was forced to be with her when he was trying to avoid her.

Might he feel she was "after" him? Or that Pastor Jim was trying to throw them together? Perhaps their closeness during the trip had, upon their return, scared him off.

Her mind replayed their conversations in the truck, but she saw nothing to explain why he would be angry with or had decided not to see her.

He never gave me reason to think I meant more to him than any other member of the group, she told herself firmly. *I must have read too much into his gentleness— rubbing my back to loosen tight muscles; stopping for me on the way to meals; including me in clowning.*

And when he hugged me on the roof that last day, it was what we were all doing when the last nail had been driven . . .like his exuberant embracing of Alice and Myron!

She would not let this get her down.

nine

Tess wondered if Pastor Jim's frequent calls meant he was becoming interested in her as more than a friend. She hoped not. She admired and liked him as much as any man she had ever known—yet didn't feel the same about him as she did Pete. She didn't love him, though she almost wished this were possible.

She must be strong and not let herself be so disappointed, so hurt, by Pete's ignoring her.

She consciously tried to keep the coldness of Pennsylvania's January from affecting her emotions, the grayness of the season from tightening around her.

Things at the college were hectic, with pressures building among the secretarial and computer employees. Each department protested that the blame was not theirs for the missing records and she was the one who bore the brunt of this. Some days she developed unaccustomed tension headaches.

She found herself praying in the car on frosty or snowy mornings for the calmness and strength needed to keep things going smoothly and to help the transition to progress without more major problems.

And then came a day when everything seemed to go well— no blowups, no short tempers. It was almost like old times, with people laughing, sharing information about families and activities, and just enjoying each other.

On her way home, she rejoiced in the afterglow, the marvelous red, orange, and salmon of the pellucid western sky following sunset. *Thank you, Lord, for the beauty of this marvelous world You created. Thank You for caring for us and helping this day to be so pleasant. Help me, please, not to let things get me down, like my fretting over computer problems. . .and Pete.*

The Christian Education meeting went smoothly, with input by all members. As they entered the Family Activity Center, Pastor Jim was laughing with her about a humorous suggestion someone made and she wasn't thinking of Pete until their eyes met across the room.

Time stopped—as did her feet. The smile left her face. Pastor Jim turned back toward her from a step ahead, undoubtedly wondering what had happened.

She looked downward, flustered. The lace of her left shoe was coming untied so she used that to explain her stopping. She placed her foot on a nearby wooden chair and bent over to tie the shoelace.

By the time she straightened, Tess had prepared herself to participate in the fun stimulated by seeing the pictures of the trip. Except she had not known that every camera taken to Florida had snapped a picture of her on Monday night and Tuesday, when she was at her very worst!

She protested the first two, then sank down a little lower in her seat as each additional one was projected. She asked that they not show these at the Association meeting and was relieved when they agreed.

Again going through those put aside for possible use, they chose ones showing specific things they wanted emphasized. They could show only a limited number of pictures. It was even more difficult to select brief portions of videotapes.

Molly protested, "It's impossible to compress that whole marvelous week into twenty minutes!"

"Especially when we're supposed to be talking in addition to this," Krystal agreed.

Pastor Jim rubbed his jaw thoughtfully. "Let's see. . .only five of our group agreed to speak—the four of us and Krystal, who will be home that night. Okay, instead of preparing individual talks, let's go through these one more time. If you feel strongly about a particular shot, volunteer to say something about that scene and what it means to you."

Tess was pleased with the response; it would make an effective presentation. Pastor Jim and Pete, who had done the videotaping, would comment on that.

Pete got to his feet and stretched. "Anyone want a ride to the pizza parlor for a bedtime snack?"

Tess kept herself from accepting, even when Molly urged her to go along. "I've got so much to do on my Independent Studies papers," she explained. "I never learned not to overload myself."

She made a hurried exit before anyone else could ask her. It might have been different had the personal invitation come from Pete.

She was tired the next day but pleased at the amount of work she had completed the night before toward her journalism project. It was good to not have to leave work to attend classes during the January term. Daylight hours were short and she went out for her major meal at noon, leaving nice long evenings to accomplish her goals.

Molly suggested they carpool for the Association meeting, so most met at the church. Pastor Jim and Pete each had a load and Tess rode in Molly's van with a number of members who would not be speaking. Her disloyal mind suggested that if Dad had not phoned just when she was about to leave the apartment, she might have arrived in time to go with Pete. . .if he had asked her.

But he wouldn't have.

Oh, stop thinking about Pete! she scolded herself.

A buffet dinner preceded the meeting, and the Fairhills group ate around tables in one corner. Usually this bothered Tess, for one goal of a get-together like this was to mingle with people from different churches, exchanging friendship and ideas.

Tess took a seat next to Krystal, who would not be returning to college until the following week. Tess commended her on the brief skit she and Pastor Jim had presented for a Mission Moment in last Sunday's church service.

Pete sat down across from her. Cautioning herself to regard this as random positioning, she was able to converse fairly easily with him and others nearby. He inquired of her how things were going at work and asked for an update on the Independent Studies projects.

"I'm almost sure to get at least a *B* in the journalism one, since *The Courier* has agreed to publish my article. However, since this is a local paper, it won't count so much as it would if it appeared in a major publication."

"Are you trying?"

"Oh, sure. And I think I have a good chance at it. But one major problem is that my pictures were taken with color film."

Pastor Jim spoke from his position beyond Krystal. "I didn't realize that's what you needed, Tess. I'll call you with the phone number of a man I worked with doing the surveys. He was constantly taking black-and-white shots for his hometown paper. I don't know if he could let you use the ones that have already been printed, but he must have a lot more."

Several others got into the conversation before Pete offered to make contact with a friend who was features editor for a major Connecticut paper.

"That gives me a great idea," she said. "With your folks living there, the article could be about you—your having gone before, getting us interested, being largely responsible for the organization of our trip."

She had never seen him so ill at ease. "Hey, wait a minute!" He raised his hand, palm forward. "This is your article. Not about me!"

"But you're the tie-in. Without you, they might not be interested. So," Tess shrugged broadly, enjoying the opportunity of making him squirm, "either you want to help or you don't."

Molly offered, "Hey, let me help fill you in with stuff you can tell about that guy," and Pastor Jim insisted she must report how Pete took advantage of people by making them do things he decided they should.

"Like clowning," Molly suggested, and Pastor Jim added a hearty, "Amen, sister!"

"Or climbing ladders." Tess pretended a scowl in his direction.

He relaxed, recognizing their banter for what it was. Folding his hands in front of himself, Pete assumed a saintly look. "I was attempting to serve as your group's conscience."

Molly hooted. "Just what we needed—an overgrown Jimminy Cricket!"

The group spent the next ten minutes contributing stories, jokes, and tidbits that "should be included in your article about Pete." People from surrounding tables came ostensibly to visit with Pastor Jim and the others they knew from Fairhills, but Tess was sure they were drawn by the laughter and fun.

Pastor Jim was the first to excuse himself, then Pete. Looking at her watch, Tess said they had better go too. Gathering the dishes of some of the older people at their table, she took them along with her own to the pass-through into the kitchen. She stopped long enough to put on a touch of lipstick and run a comb through her hair before entering the sanctuary with Molly and Krystal.

"I wish they hadn't asked us to sit up front," Molly

grumbled.

Tess commented, "Just because you sit near the back in your home church doesn't mean you have to do the same here, Molly."

"I started that when my kids were little, so they wouldn't distract other people, and it just stuck."

They sat in the second pew, with Pete and Pastor Jim. There was congregational singing, a small amount of business, a few announcements, an offering, a sermonette or devotional and it was time for their presentation.

They had agreed that Pastor Jim should take care of the preliminaries. He did this with his usual skill and poise so in a few minutes, pictures, beginning with October's dinner at Fairhills, began appearing on the large screen.

Pete was introduced as a major influence on what took place and Pastor Jim asked him up front to help show by photo and word how things were organized and scheduled. Pictures of the truck's being loaded with donated supplies, the group's leaving the morning after Christmas, and the stopover in South Carolina were shown.

Pastor Jim explained, "These next shots were taken by a friend who had the opportunity of seeing things from a helicopter. There are all degrees of damage, from here in Homestead—which was so very badly hit, as you've seen countless times on your TV screens—and this area where the fronts are off of some of these condominiums."

"Partial responsibility for a lot of the excessive damage, like here," Pete said, "was the way they were built. Notice how whole sections of the front just peeled away, showing the kitchen cupboards and refrigerators and bathtubs. It's almost like looking into a dollhouse. We were told that if they'd been constructed properly, this wouldn't have been nearly as bad."

Tess, Molly, and Krystal were standing now, also, and joined in commenting briefly about scenes projected on the screen. Tess thought she had seen Pastor Jim's pictures often enough to not be unduly affected, but she had to clear her throat as she explained that the crushed aluminum wrapped around that tree represented not only the loss of the man's home and possessions, but of his grandson.

She also found it hard to speak of the little barefoot girl crying in the wreckage of her house, too frightened and unhappy to make her way back out through the splintered wood, broken glass, and jagged metal to find her mother.

Molly explained about their work on the roofs. "We were involved only with those that were salvageable. Some, like this one, needed just to have these loosened shingles removed and then to have them and the missing ones replaced. These more severely damaged roofs required major reconstruction—replacing beams, like here, and putting on new sheathing before we could begin replacing shingles."

Krystal told them, "I couldn't imagine why we brought flat-tined potato forks with us but you can see here what we did with them. I'm the one on the right, ripping off those shingles—and discovering muscles I didn't know I had, work.

"These cement shingles make a lot of sense in southern

Florida and would have continued doing a good job had not the wood under them been riddled by termites. There was nothing to hold them on, so even a lesser hurricane than Andrew would probably have loosened them."

Tess gasped with horror to discover they had inserted a picture of her in the secretary's office! As she covered her face with her hands, Molly explained, "Tess is upset that we're showing her when, to put it mildly, she doesn't look too great. I asked that one be included and this is the best shot of her during a several-day period."

Tess groaned, then punched her lightly on the shoulder. Molly went on telling briefly of the asthma attack, its cause, and of Tess's determination to keep going, which led to her programming the church's computer. "This is only one example of the dedication of each volunteer to the mission and of their willingness to use whatever skills were most needed.

"There was also our Pastor Jim who expected to rip off shingles and pound nails, but spent most of his time doing the surveys necessary to set up work sites for volunteers following us. But you tell them about that, Pastor."

Following the slides and the men's narration of the video, there was an informal period of questions and answers. People crowded around them for another forty-five minutes after the session closed, asking for more information and making comments.

A middle-aged woman shared with Tess her own experiences with mold-triggered asthma and another came to relate her harrowing computer problems and how she had solved them.

Pete's long strides brought him to her side as she stepped onto the parking lot. "So your papers are coming along well, Tess?"

"Fairly well, thanks. I still have a lot to do, but I should meet my deadlines." She smiled up at him. "I'd like to have that editor's name. Could you give it to me, now?"

"I could, but," he stood still and she turned to see him looking troubled, "don't make the article about me."

"But—"

"Please."

"Why not? You aren't that modest!"

"I'm not trying to be modest, Tess. Or difficult."

"But you're my best selling point for a Connecticut paper, Pete. Won't you reconsider?"

"There are. . .reasons why I'd rather not."

He obviously had decided not to discuss those reasons, but she had to ask, "Could I at least mention your name and your enthusiastic challenge to our church? That's what got us to go to Florida. It's my only tie-in with that paper."

The others had moved on to their vehicles and nobody interrupted what they must have recognized as a serious discussion. "Perhaps—wouldn't it be better to try an in-state newspaper?"

Her eyes narrowed. Why was she in the position of having to plead for something he had suggested in the first place? She adopted a teasing tone. "Did you get run out of town or something? Are you hiding out in our safe little Fairhills?"

He looked startled but then grinned, and they started walking again, he with his hands deep in his pockets. "Nothing that exciting, I assure you. However, there's plenty to write about the rest of them."

She was disappointed that he didn't ask her to ride back in his car. But why had she even thought he might? He already has a load, you idiot. *And Molly's over there patiently waiting for you in her van.*

The next day, she went to the college library at noon and found there was only one major paper in his hometown. She wrote down the feature editor's name and number but didn't get through the first time she called. She was pleased when, in midafternoon, a businesslike voice answered with, "Allyson Kaiser speaking."

Tess introduced herself and her purpose. There was a noticeable warming in the other's manner when told that Peter Macfarland had suggested his hometown paper as a possibility for this article. "I am interested in seeing it but amazed he suggested it. He always claimed he didn't like being in the limelight."

"That is a problem," Tess confessed. "He doesn't want anything in the feature about himself, even though I explained that his part in our project could be the one reason you might consider this."

"What would he say if you told him you were right?"

Tess paused. He would be angry—at least disappointed and annoyed—to know she had made this contact. He had deliberately withheld this woman's name and number. "You won't consider the article if he's not in it?"

"Oh, I'll look at it. But Pete's the connection I'd like, since he's a local man. Another thing, do you have good pictures?"

"I think so. However, they're all color prints, so if you need black-and-white ones, I can borrow them."

"Is there a photo supply store nearby? Often, they have someone on staff who could make glossies from your negatives."

"I don't know. I'll check."

Ms. Kaiser was apparently trying to be helpful. "Do that, but in the meantime send good photocopies of the color prints you think might supplement your writing. Identify the pictures on all the sheets and be sure to keep copies of the pages in case I should ask for glossies."

Tess needed to make sure she understood. "So I should wait to have black-and-white prints made till I hear from you?"

"Right. But I'd personally like you to include a couple of your color shots with Pete in them." She then asked, "When will you mail the manuscript?"

"Tomorrow. And one more thing: Our pastor has some excellent color photos. Might I send copies of his, as well?"

The editor didn't seem to mind her additional questions. Her voice was still warm. "Put his on sheets separate from yours and mark them accordingly. That way I'll know if he needs to sign a release, and we can send payment to him.

Your pictures, of course, would be considered part of the manuscript package."

Tess was grateful for this deadline; it would force her to discipline herself. She used every moment of the evening to rewrite and polish, and finally completed the task.

She had stopped at the parsonage on her way home that day and picked up the pictures Pastor Jim good-naturedly gave permission to use. When she returned them the following day, she left photocopies, though she considered these poor reproductions of his brilliant originals. They should, however, serve to give the editor some indication of what was available.

Tess smiled as she entered the apartment and walked through to the kitchen. It was good to be able to see the uncluttered top of the cherry table again. She started to put her jacket over the back of a chair, then carried it to the closet and hung it on a hanger. Just because she had cleared away one mess didn't mean she should start another! But she did, of course.

After dinner she got out the file of materials for her paper on volunteers. She hadn't looked at this collection of notes for the last four days. Now, she saw more clearly the wealth of material she had. A smile established residence on her face; this could be better than she had anticipated.

It was true it needed much work, but the organization of data was sound. More formal and less colorful than the article she had mailed today, it was still very readable, and accurate.

The ending, however, needed to be more concise. Taking with her some notes she had made on the back of an envelope, Tess went to the computer to try various ideas. Two hours later, she shut down the system and stretched. She was satisfied with the last revision—as of now. It might not look as good in the morning, but she was going to bed.

Sunday school went smoothly. That wasn't always the case since one of the girls and two of the boys often tried to see how far they could go to disrupt their class. Luther, the ringleader, was not there and Tess had to silently ask forgiveness for the fleeting thought that his absence was a blessing. If anyone in the class needed Christian teaching, it was Luther.

One of the kids chose to stay and talk as Tess was always willing to do. Today, however, it made her almost late getting to church. She took an aisle seat a little more than halfway toward the front. The organist had begun his music when Tess felt a firm hand on her shoulder and heard a whispered comment, "I thought you weren't sending that article to Connecticut."

A welcoming smile started when Tess first heard his voice but left as she turned. She greeted him with a whispered, "Good morning, Pete," before she realized how grim he looked.

His head jerked downward in a nod of acknowledgment of her words, not of approval. "Allyson tells me she received your manuscript."

"You're the one who suggested it, Pete," she defended herself. "And you didn't say I couldn't send it if I left you out of it."

"But you didn't!" His voice carried a sting, even though whispered.

"I wrote, 'A man who recently joined First Church.' I didn't identify you."

"The pictures did. I'm apparently in a bunch of them."

"I didn't offer any pictures of you for publication."

His brown eyes continued looking into her blue ones for an uncomfortably long time. What could she say if he didn't respond? She was almost relieved when he yanked a hymn book from the rack in front of him and, leaning back against his pew, pointedly began reading.

Could she move back to the empty space beside him? Was he angry enough—or disappointed enough—to get up and leave if she did? For that matter, what would she do if he chose to ignore her completely?

You've created a horrible situation, Tess, she told herself. *You set your judgement and personal goals against what you sensed he disapproved of—and you lost. Now what?*

Tess kept tugging her mind back to the service, but when it was over she couldn't remember any of the hymns and hardly knew what the sermon was about. This troubled her more than she could have expected; not only had she let herself get bogged down with uncertainties and feeling miserable about Pete, but she had permitted that to keep God's Word and the message of His servant from getting through to her.

She would turn around and apologize as soon as the benediction was pronounced—but Pete was gone. He must have moved into the aisle even before Pastor Jim said, "Amen," for he was already at the door, shaking hands with the pastor, one of the first to leave.

So be it. She wasn't going to let it bother her. *See if I care about your rudeness, Peter Macfarland!* She was glowering on the inside. Could the fake smile on her face cover her confusion and hurt? She left the church quickly and hurried to her car.

Why had he called Allyson? Or why should Allyson have called him about the article? The thought that there might be something between them filled her with anger, but whether more at herself or him was a question.

An irregular pattern of snowflakes floated in the air, appearing not to be falling but moving in an erratic dance about her. *They're like my thoughts, the same ones flying by over and over, not settling down into anything that counts.*

She stopped to pick up Sunday's *Philadelphia Inquirer* and a carton of milk. She thought of getting a hoagie or pizza but had no enthusiasm for either. Leftovers would do.

Vehicles filled the spaces along her street in front of her apartment so Tess parked around the corner. Quick steps brought her almost to her door before she heard Pete's voice.

Her feet stopped of their own volition and she turned as

he approached. "Tess," he was troubled, uncertain. "I need to apologize for acting that way. Can you forgive me?"

She was the one who should be saying she was sorry. Taken by surprise, she asked, "For what, Pete?"

His face was an abject study. "I was angry when Allyson told me last night about your manuscript package arriving. But the house of God is the last place where I should confront you about it—if I have a right to do so at all."

She didn't know what to say, but nodded when he asked if he could come in. The cold didn't feel nearly as severe now, even with its swirling gusts of wind.

Tess unlocked and opened her door and they went inside. "Can I hang up your coat?"

"No, thanks. I'll just lay it here on the couch for a minute—if that's okay."

So he was expecting to leave soon. "Can you stay for ham-and-cheese sandwiches, tomato soup, and fruit?"

He apparently intended to decline, for he stammered, "I. . .think it's better n. . .," then changed his mind. "Uh, well, yes, if it's not too much trouble."

"That's what I plan to eat." She led the way to the kitchen, grateful she had mopped the white-on-white floor and cleared away the overflow of her projects from the pale wood counters. As she put bread, lettuce, mayonnaise, relishes, and sliced meat and cheese on the counter, Pete used the electric can opener then dumped the can's contents and some water into a pan. He put plates, glasses, silverware, and napkins on the table, then, as the soup began to simmer, added milk.

Tess was afraid to say anything that could make the conversation even more strained than it already was. It was after their tea was in front of them at the end of lunch that he asked, "Please tell me what Allyson said when you called."

She had not expected this direct a question. "She seemed willing to look at what I'd written, but no guarantee of buying it. She also implied there would be little chance that she would if you weren't included."

"And that's why you sent the pictures?"

"I sent mostly photocopies of my color prints and some of Pastor Jim's. Those that have you in them are the best ones to illustrate the article, but they were not offered for that purpose. She asked me to send a few prints of you— out of personal interest, I assumed."

Pete's questions made her uneasy. "Now I'll ask you something, Pete. Why does this trouble you so much?"

His gaze dropped to his hands, which were slowly rotating the mug between his palms—forward a little, then back. "Good question." His lips thinned as they pressed together for a moment. "And you deserve an honest answer."

ten

Pete straightened on his chair. "Allyson and I have dated ever since high school. During college it was off and on. Once we agreed it might be a good idea to go out with others. And then she married a real jerk right after graduation."

Tess felt her eyelids twitch. *Something connected with Allyson is why he never said or did anything to lead me on. I was too stupid to realize it. But he was in his upper twenties and. . . .* "And you. . .were you married?"

"No. I've never been married. And her marriage lasted a total of just over two months. I tried helping her through the emotional trauma of learning that Hank was unfaithful—even during their honeymoon, as it turned out. She couldn't believe he didn't love her."

"How awful for her!"

"Yes."

She leaned forward on her arms, crossed on the table before her. "Pete?" It seemed a long time before his dark eyes met hers. "Is she still grieving over that?"

"It did terrible things to her self-esteem and to her emotional and social well-being. I tried to get her into Christian counseling, but she'd never admit she needed it. She was by then a feature writer for the paper—and very good at it. Being promoted several times, now to features editor, she's convinced she's handled everything wonderfully."

"She's all right now?"

"Professionally, yes; emotionally, no. For one thing, she's become. . .very possessive."

That explained some things. "You still feel responsible for her?"

His smile was crooked. "It sounds sick, doesn't it? Maybe it is. By the way, she wants us to get married."

By the way, he'd said. As though this were a minor matter. The tightness in her chest made it difficult to breathe. She managed, "You're engaged?"

"That, too, is a good question. Allyson thinks so; I don't. I never asked her to marry me and haven't given her a ring. I avoid discussing houses and. . .and things like that which she keeps bringing up.

"I was unbelievably relieved to get this teaching job, hoping that if I weren't there all the time she'd develop more strength within herself. . .would find someone else to lean on."

"Has it worked?"

"Not enough to mention. I drove back the first few weekends, but not anymore."

"Did you go because you wanted to?"

He had not drunk much of his tea, which must be tepid by now. He took a sip before answering. "I felt she still needed me and, well, it didn't seem unreasonable. It really isn't too far to travel. But as I got acquainted with people,

I wanted to be here on weekends. For one thing, I became aware of you my first Sunday at Fairhills, though I had no opportunity to talk with you until that October dinner."

"I remember."

"And then the Thanksgiving dinner. . .and Christmas . . .and the trip to Florida. Each time I was with you I came to like and respect you more. But I felt. . .almost guilty."

"Do you love her?"

He drew in a deep breath. "As a dear friend whom I've known for a long time. We've been through many experiences and our lives have been. . .intertwined on many levels."

His right forefinger traced the pattern in the lace cover she had placed on the table. "But as for being in love? No, Tess, I'm not."

"But you've thought about marrying her?" It was difficult to ask this question that filled her with a pain she hoped he couldn't read in her eyes.

He covered her hand with his. "I've thought about it in the past. . .but can't consider it anymore."

Please, God, make him go on. It isn't right for me to ask questions on anything this personal.

"Allyson wanted to know all about you—how old you are, how pretty, how smart. And what our relationship is, whether we kiss or anything."

It was Tess's turn to break eye contact as she felt the flush staining her cheeks. Pete held her hand more tightly as she started to pull it away. "I answered her questions, Tess. But when she again begged me to set our marriage date, I put her off.

"It's impossible for me to consider doing that. I can't marry without the First Corinthians, chapter thirteen, kind of love. . .and knowing that my spouse feels the same way."

Tess's throat was so tight she could hardly manage, "I'm sure you can't, Pete."

"But I'm sure she isn't strong enough yet to handle my coming right out and telling her."

Nothing was resolved when he left. Tess was in turmoil as she leaned her head against the door after they had said good night. It was almost as if he had asked her advice about marrying another woman! And he loved Allyson, even if he qualified that as not being the First Corinthians, chapter thirteen, kind of love.

As for herself? Tess pushed herself upright and headed for the kitchen. While she washed their few dishes, she recognized that the only thing he had said about his feelings toward her were that he "liked" and "respected" her.

And yet, if that were really the only response she engendered, would he have come here like this? Would he have told her even as much as he had?

The next morning, she called Allyson Kaiser to withdraw the manuscript from consideration. The editor had already decided to "go with it." It would appear in Sunday's feature section. With lots of pictures!

"You have nearly a week to get something else," Tess

protested, hardly caring if Allyson considered this begging.

Allyson's voice showed a firmness Tess hadn't heard before. "You obviously know nothing of what goes into each week's paper. And I had every reason to believe you were offering it for publication when you sent it."

"I was." She had to admit to that. "But I've reconsidered. It would be better for an in-state paper."

"You received a better offer." It was a statement, not a question.

Tess hadn't considered this interpretation. "Nobody else has seen it. This was not a simultaneous submission. It's just that. . . ." How could she possibly explain something that didn't make sense to her? "Pete does not want any pictures used that include him."

Allyson's laugh didn't sound quite right to Tess, and her words didn't either, though they could have been meant as reassurance. "Don't worry about Pete. I can handle him. I always do."

Do you? Really? Tess looked at the phone, eyes narrowed. "Perhaps you can, Miss Kaiser," she said softly, then added with all the honesty in her heart, "but I don't want to."

"Sorry. It's too late to make the change."

"It can't be. You don't have my photographs."

"You forget you sent some sample shots along with those copies. We'll make do with these. Unless you send additional ones."

"Wouldn't it be too late to get them to you in time?" She

didn't care if the editor heard her sarcasm. She didn't appreciate Allyson's deliberately trying to get her in trouble with Pete.

The response was patronizing. "Don't take this personally, Miss Kenneman. If you continue writing, you'll learn that things aren't always what you want in publishing."

Tess controlled an almost overwhelming urge to retort angrily. She forced her voice to remain calm as she requested one more time, "I would appreciate your returning the unpublished manuscript, Miss Kaiser."

"Impossible. We will, however, return your photographs with your check, following publication. If I were you, I'd be grateful for this exposure but don't expect me to accept anything else of yours. Ever."

The sound of the phone's being returned to its cradle was loud in Tess's ear. Well, she had tried. She didn't know whether Pete would believe her—or whether she would even have an opportunity to tell him what had transpired.

If only she had settled for the article in the local paper with its *B*-plus! Or perhaps she could have gotten it into a Harrisburg or Philadelphia paper if she had tried. But no, she had gone against Pete's wishes and sent it to his old girlfriend—the woman who considered herself his fiancée.

When she got home from work, she picked up the file folder in which she kept all her material on the trip to Florida. Riffling through pages, she reread portions of what she had put in her laptop computer there at the church in Florida. She hadn't realized how often Pete's name and activities were mentioned.

Over an hour later, her leg asleep from being curled under her on the couch, she became aware that she was no longer angry or even sad. She was thankful for the opportunity she had had of going with the group to fix those houses—and help with the computer—and do the clowning.

It might even be a good thing that the report of this adventure was going to be read in Connecticut next Sunday. If she were a relative or friend of Pete's, she would enjoy reading of what he had accomplished.

So there, Miss Allyson Kaiser! She was smiling as she limped to the kitchen to microwave the homemade soup that had been defrosting in the refrigerator.

Sunday again. Sunday school and church. She sat back farther in the congregation so she could see if Pete was there.

He was. Her eyes feasted on the sight of his broad shoulders, his muscled neck, the brown, slightly wavy hair irregularly bleached from his rooftop work in Florida.

What was he thinking, this man whom she had once thought she knew well? He joined in the singing and the responsive reading. He smiled as he passed the offering plate to the woman on his left. . .and sour old Miss Henderson smiled back. Tess's lips curved upward, too, remembering how good it felt to have that open approval and genuine liking fastened on herself.

She looked down at the Bible on her lap, eyes closing

with the pain which that thought brought by being in the past. Did those smiles for her belong only to the past?

She wished there were some way she could get a copy of the paper in which her article was appearing. Allyson had said they would send her tear sheets, but would she, now that she was angry? If so, when would she receive them? The Connecticut paper wasn't one of the many carried in the college or town library. She had looked in both places before sending the manuscript, wanting to check their format, to make sure hers conformed.

Tess wondered if Nancy Rohrer, her college roommate, might get it. Although she lived in northern Connecticut, it was possible.

She was doing the same thing as last week—not paying attention to the service! Intrigued with the title of Pastor Jim's sermon, "And Then What?" when she saw it in the bulletin, she had already missed the first half of it but now winced, recognizing herself in what he was saying.

"Everyone keeps trying to box in the Lord, telling Him what He should be doing, and how. If things don't go exactly that way, we try second guessing Him as to why He's not accommodating our wisdom."

Tess's lips turned upward wryly as he requested people to look back over just this last day, week, and month to review what they had asked for and what had been received. "Perhaps there are things you'd still like to be otherwise. Things like illness, death, loss of a job—major things. Or for a friend to call."

Her errant thoughts made her lose track of the sermon

again. When she pulled them back, he was asking if there were happenings during that period which had seemed coincidental or lucky, or perhaps too small to worry about.

These might be seeds that would grow and develop into something better than what was requested. Perhaps they hadn't yet borne fruit, needing more time to mature. He mentioned the Apostle Paul, who had excellent reasons to go one way until God changed his plans. He reminded them that those who traveled with Jesus for three years expected to be rewarded in His earthly kingdom.

He mentioned Lincoln and Ulysses Grant and a famous baseball player—three men who had suffered terrible setbacks that changed their careers and lives.

Pastor Jim challenged them to keep looking for God's hand in things around them—to seek, for they would surely find. And he suggested that when these things were made clear, it would be good to share not only the results but the struggles with others who might be wondering and doubting.

"Your witness is needed more than mine. Many feel that as a pastor I'm paid to give encouragement and it's to my personal advantage to keep you contented. They can't shrug off as easily your going out on a limb to tell of your relationship with God."

I'm lax in this, Tess admitted. *Even when I talk about our experiences in Florida, I don't always give credit for how God took care of us. . .and got us doing things we didn't know we were going to. . .and provided friendships. . . .*

She slowly bowed her head and closed her eyes. *Dear Lord, I do thank You for all of these, especially the friendships. Help me in maintaining them. Even with Pete, Lord, help me be more willing to keep just friendship, if that's all that's offered. It's true I want more than that, but only You know if that's best for both of us.*

At the end of the service, as she turned to leave her pew, she saw Dad and Jeannette across the aisle and three rows back. She went to hug each of them and, while they were talking, heard that beloved voice, "Mr. and Mrs. Kenneman, it's good to see you here this morning."

Pete didn't say the same to her, not in words anyway, but Tess welcomed his warm hand upon her left shoulder and his arm around her back as he reached around to shake their hands.

Dad greeted him. "We were about to ask Tess to join us for dinner at Semper's Turkey Ranch. Are you free to come with us—either there or some place you like better?"

"Okay with you?" he asked Tess as casually as though they had been seeing one another regularly.

"Sounds good to me." Very, very good!

"How about the women riding in the back?" Dad suggested. Pete was enthusiastically admiring his new Chrysler and continued asking questions about it.

Tess would have preferred Pete's sitting with her, but it really didn't matter. There was conversation among all four of them on the fifteen-minute drive to the sprawling one-story restaurant with its two added-on wings.

As would be expected, poultry was the specialty.

Jeannette chose steak tips but the other three ordered the all-you-can-eat dinner of turkey and waffles. While waiting to be served, there was an easy give-and-take in catching up with one another's activities.

Her father was modernizing one of the two bathrooms in his free time. Jeannette, in addition to helping with that, had begun stenciling around the top of the walls in the hallway, having finished those in the living room.

Pete had volunteered to work with the elementary school's basketball program. Their regular practice included early Wednesday evenings, precluding his attendance at Bible study.

Tess told about her two college projects. She was getting an *A* on the first and expected the same on the second.

Pete's dark eyes seemed locked on hers. "It's in the Connecticut paper?"

She hoped her stomach spasm wasn't reflected on her face. "It should be in today's issue." Tearing her gaze from his, she explained to the others, "I needed to get it into a publication outside of the local area in order to be given a higher grade. Pete suggested I submit it to a paper covering his home district and. . .the editor agreed."

She tried to go on, to explain she had attempted to get it back, but her father immediately jumped in with thanks for Pete's efforts on his daughter's behalf. It had to be deliberate that Pete avoided meeting her gaze and quickly changed the topic of conversation.

Other than that, the meal went smoothly. Once the food

was in front of them and Pete prayed, he talked with her as freely as with the others and she hoped that indicated he was no longer angry.

I should have known better! she told herself later when, getting out of the car with Pete when Dad dropped him by his parked Grand Am, she attempted to explain what had happened.

"Look," he said, interrupting her, "I knew it was in. Allyson called last night to 'congratulate' me on how handsome I look in the photos."

"I want to tell you—"

His head jerked from side to side. "You have, Tess. You wanted an *A*."

She flinched as though she had been slapped. "You've got to listen, Pete. I tried. I really tried to get the article back. That and the pictures."

"After it was too late to do anything about it."

"I didn't know it was too late. I called Monday morning—as soon as I could—when I realized how very unhappy this whole stupid thing made you!"

His sigh was heavy; his voice, tired. "Okay, Tess. It's over now. Let's just leave it."

What was over, the article's being printed in the paper or—please, God, no—their friendship? "I didn't think it was right to call her at home even if I had known her number, which I didn't."

He was getting into his car, not looking at her. She wondered what he would think about Allyson's stating she could always "handle" him. But that was irrelevant. Tess wouldn't tell him; it wasn't her place to do so. And Allyson certainly wouldn't!

At least he hadn't slammed the door shut to emphasize his displeasure. She slipped off her glove and touched the back of her right hand against his left cheek. It was cool to her touch and she risked getting an even colder response as she ventured, "Ever since last Sunday, Pete, I can honestly say I'd rather have that promised *B*-plus than an *A* received at the cost of our friendship. Had I known of any way to retrieve the manuscript, it would have been done."

"You might have called me."

"I couldn't."

"Why not?"

"Because. . ." how could she explain this? "If she considers herself your fianceé, how could I possibly go over her head to complain to you?" she blurted out, unshed tears burning her eyes.

He continued looking through the windshield. She removed her hand from the physical contact and unseeingly pushed it into her still warm leather glove. Turning on her heel, she ran up the street to her car.

Quickly, she got in and rushed through the buckling up routine. She started the faithful Civic and pulled out without glancing back in his direction.

Home. She should be relaxing and enjoying the novelty of having free time on a Sunday afternoon. No homework. No articles. No research.

But no Pete!

Her week was hectic. Problems with the transferral of data again. She prayed for guidance through much of Tuesday night, asking what she could do at work—and also how she should resolve or begin to smooth the situation with Pete.

She got up early and sat by the eastern window, praying for wisdom. The brightening took place so slowly there was no point at which she could say "This is darkness" or "This is light." *Is this what You want me to remember, Lord—that I should let things happen gradually?* But that's what she had been trying to do and everything had fallen apart.

Am I to remember that You are the only true Light? She knew and acknowledged that. *What else, Lord? What else should I be learning? What should I do? What can I say to make things better?*

She had enough questions—answers eluded her.

The upper edge of the sun was nibbling an arc of slate from the house roof across the street. She got to her feet and headed for the shower, saying out loud, "Perhaps You want me to know that the sun—and You and Your Son— are always there, even when I can only see the effects, not the substance."

eleven

The phone was ringing as she came through the door but the line went dead as she put it to her ear. Alicia came in, looking worried. "Good morning, Tess—at least I hope it is. I was just handed a memo from the president's office."

Tess reached for the cream-colored sheet. It was a short message, straight to the point. "A special meeting is being held in his office at eleven," she told her secretary. "I'm to be there."

"Is it about the missing information?"

"Probably." Tess tried for a smile. "Who knows what's going to happen? I'm still praying about that."

She discouraged further speculation on the subject but wondered who had been on the phone as she arrived. Might it have been a personal call, someone she could have asked to pray for her? Probably not, for she discouraged personal calls here.

Would she have asked for prayers had it been someone like Pastor Jim? Or Molly? Or Pete? But it couldn't have been him. If it would have been possible to request prayers had Pastor Jim or Molly called her, could she phone one of them?

Molly would be at work. So would Pastor Jim, but his "work" was largely made up of talking with people. She rang the church and the secretary put her through to the inner office. "Good morning. Pastor Hadden speaking. Can I help you?"

"Yes, Pastor Jim, I think you can. This is Tess and I'm calling to ask if you'd pray for me."

His warm voice was reassuring. "I have been, Tess, and will continue doing that. Is there something special— some specific need right now?"

"I...yes there is. I'm at the college and things are falling apart here."

"In getting the material on the computer? Like what you spoke of on the trip?"

She had been afraid he would have forgotten that conversation. She sketched, in a few sentences, the added problem of missing records, telling as much as she could without breaking trust concerning her job.

He asked, "Have you ever seen this missing information? Is it something that was on the computer and is now lost. . .or was it never there?"

"I've never seen it. I suspect it wasn't put on when the system was updated. And yet—I really shouldn't be talking about this."

"I understand." He then asked if she, personally, was in trouble.

She told of the meeting coming up this morning. She supposed she could even lose her job over discrepancies in the endowment funds, although she was the one who had found and reported the problem.

"May I put this on the prayer chain?"

"I. . .think not." She would have liked having more prayers, but the fewer people who knew of this problem, the better. "However, you can tell anyone you run into that I need their prayers."

She kept busy with routine things. Her hand fumbled for the ringing phone some time later. "Tess Kenneman speaking."

She sat up straight, her world tilting somewhat more toward its normal axis as her friend's voice said, "Good morning, Tess. This is Molly. Pastor Jim tells me you're in a jam. Anything I can do?"

"Where are you?"

"At work. He came to my office, knowing I'd want that."

"I. . .appreciate your concern. And Pastor Jim's. More than you can imagine."

"He was going to tell Pete, also. . .to ask for prayer."

"I'm. . .starting to cry," she confessed, fishing in her desk drawer for tissues.

"Wait for that till the tears can be from relief—after your meeting," the firm voice advised.

Tess heard her own sniffle through the phone and apologized, "I'm sorry. . .but I'm so worried!"

"You're not in this alone, Tess. Remember that."

"I will. I really will." She swallowed hard and looked at the large wall clock. "I must leave in about twenty-five minutes, so I'm especially grateful you called when you did."

"And the meeting is when?"

"In about thirty. . .thirty-two minutes."

"I won't hold you. Go wash your eyes with cold water or whatever you need to do, then go over there and wow them!" There was an almost humorous note in her voice as she said that, but the final statement was dead serious. "We'll take care of the praying part for you."

How wonderful that Molly cared and was supportive! Along with all the other stresses, Tess now felt guilty about that, too, for she hadn't made enough effort to stay in close touch with this woman she had come to admire and love.

But Molly wouldn't want her worrying about that.

She took her purse to the women's room and put on lipstick before returning to her computer, notes from conversations with the comptroller, treasurer, finance chairman, and the head of the computer department lying on the desk beside it.

Twice she refused to accept on-campus calls as her fingers raced across the keys. She printed out what she had written and took that to the photocopier.

Picking up the folder of memos and records she had gathered previously, she added the sheets from the copier and left the building. She was hardly aware of the cold as she walked across the open quadrangle to Old Main.

Tess pulled open the heavy white steel-and-glass door and walked in. Several individuals hurried toward her, asking questions and assuring her that whatever had happened had not been their fault. She put them off with, "Let's wait till we get in his office."

She commiserated with the office manager over her

two-month-old daughter's getting days and nights mixed up. Gerald Mosseau, the comptroller, accepted congratulations on his paper that had just come out in a professional journal and that reminded a secretary to tell Tess how much she had enjoyed the article on the Florida trip that had appeared in the local paper.

Dr. Joseph Popler's appearance exemplified what Tess would have envisioned for a university president. Nearly six-feet tall, he carried himself erectly and wore perfectly tailored suits. In his late fifties, he retained a full head of salt-and-pepper hair that always looked the same, never a hair out of place. His intelligent hazel eyes appeared to see everything.

The right number of chairs, five, were arranged in a semicircle before his large, carved walnut desk. Tess found herself in the center seat, which she would never have chosen. She suspected it had been maneuvered.

Even Dr. Popler's patience was tried as Mr. Mosseau and another department head loudly disclaimed any responsibility for the missing financial records. The president stepped in several times to insist that only one person speak at a time, and then asked a few questions.

He repeated their complaints in a few short sentences, showing he understood the problem. He then turned toward her. "And you, Miss Kenneman. What do you have to say about this?"

She had been afraid she would be tongue-tied before him but the words came easily as she explained she had been following orders in working toward getting material on the new system within the specified time.

She recounted her discovery of some missing accounts, some missing names, then waited until interruptions were taken care of. Mr. Mosseau angrily implied that she was incompetent and libelous and suggested she be replaced.

"Replaced? By whom?" Dr. Popler asked brusquely. "She's one of our most respected computer experts and has done nothing unprofessional or unpleasant. She had to notify you and me of discrepancies; that's hardly an accusation of anyone in your or any other department."

Tess was grateful he had said that, but she still couldn't relax. She had no opportunity to speak again for a few minutes, until Dr. Popler directly addressed her. "You've apparently checked all the material you have, Miss Kenneman. How do you suggest handling things at this point?"

"I'm still hoping it proves to be simply a matter of differences in the way information was recorded within departments. We've begun an intensive search of individual and corporate donors in relation to the dates on which gifts were received and we're exploring other possibilities."

She handed out copies of how each department had cooperated thus far and what was in process. "In one of these areas I've highlighted, there's got to be misfiled hard or soft copy records. In our section, we're putting in any time we can spare—plus much of our own—to search for information, mostly for improperly recorded entries prior to the last computer updating. I suggest that all departments do that."

There was near silence for a minute or two before several changes in the wording were made, but none to the content of the reports.

"Take this back to your departments," Dr. Popler said. "Get your colleagues involved with the search and assure them there's no penalty for an honest mistake. With changes of responsibility through the years, it's a marvel something like this hasn't come to light before."

He flipped open his appointment book and poised his pen above it. "Return here at the same time next week. In the meantime, I'll listen to suggestions. But only if they come in a positive way—if they clarify and are not made," his smile was mirthless, "to obfuscate."

Tess tried to keep her face from showing humor at his deliberate choice of that word. It contained a warning to not hide behind things confusing or "academic."

They were dismissed as surely as though he had stated this. There was something about his demeanor as he stood beside his desk that discouraged their lingering to visit or rehash. Tess stepped aside to allow the others to precede her, but glanced back as she started to follow them. His right hand lifted from the shiny desk top in the hint of a salute and his lips parted to form an almost silent, "Thank you."

Her smile was genuine. Giving a slow nod that was almost a little bow, she left the room. *It has to be those prayers that kept me calm before and through that meeting.*

She would call Molly and Pastor Jim as soon as she got back to her office.

But she didn't.

Her walk back was more free and joyous than it had been less than an hour before. She ran up the steps of her building, across the porch, through the door—and collided with a tall man standing there reading notices on the overcrowded bulletin board. "Oh, I'm sorry. . .," she started, then gasped, "Pete! What are you doing here?"

He had reached to steady her, holding her so close his breath was warm against her face. "I can tell you don't need my shoulder to cry on."

She would always want those shoulders. Did he know that? "Don't you have school today?"

He nodded but continued searching her eyes with his beautiful brown ones. "I had to know you're all right. Pastor Jim came to tell me you were worried about the outcome of your meeting. I want you to know you had—you have—my prayers. All the time."

His voice was husky. "I wish you had called me."

"I would have liked to." How did she have courage to say that after his not contacting her?

It felt as though he was pulling her closer but she must have been mistaken for he then released her. "In less than fifteen minutes I must be in school with my children. When do you finish?"

It was his lunch time then that he was using to be with her. "How about you?"

"Probably four-thirty. A parent's coming to talk with

me after he gets off work."

"I'll be home by then."

His large hands cupped her face, fingers caressing her ears then tangling in her hair. "I'll see you then."

She continued to feel his touch long after he left her to hurry back to his pupils. She walked slowly to her office, no longer in a hurry to share news of the meeting. What seemed to be happening with Pete seemed far more important—and private.

She ate lunch with coworkers at the Student Union building and nobody mentioned it if she occasionally drifted into a world of her own. Often at noon she would get a full meal then fix just a sandwich and salad in the evening. Today she ate little. She hoped Pete and she would be together for dinner. He would be hungry since he had missed lunch.

Time toyed with her through the afternoon, going slowly yet not allowing opportunity to get much accomplished. She was usually the last to leave—today she was the first.

She straightened the few things that were out of place in her apartment, including the dishes she had put in the drainer to dry. She had planned to call Pastor Jim, to report on the meeting, but there wasn't time before Pete was at her door.

In response to his knock on the door, she hurried across the room then stood there, savoring the moment, eager yet shy. She ran her palms down over the front of her slim wool skirt and opened the door to the man she loved. It was so good having him here, tall and handsome and wonderful. "Pete!" She reached out both hands. "Come in."

He held them in his, pressing them to his heart. "I'm glad you said that."

"You couldn't have doubted I would."

"Well, I did give you warning." His smile was fleeting, however light his words. He closed the door and led the way to the couch.

The sun had not set but Tess suddenly wished she had turned on a lamp or two. His eyes seemed shadowed as he said, "Tell me about your meeting."

Tess had almost forgotten the meeting in her anticipation of what might occur now, but briefly explained what had taken place. He continued holding her right hand tightly as he asked specific questions.

She finally protested, "That's enough about me. Tell me about your day—or week—or whatever."

He faced her directly. "I'll start with Sunday afternoon—after dinner and what you said there at my car. I realized how miserably I've been treating you."

"It's all right, Pete."

"No." His head shake was emphatic. "It isn't. You've been far more patient than I deserve. First, I try to help you, then am angry because you take my advice. You try to straighten things out and I jump down your throat. Why do you put up with me, Theresa?"

She should give some reason other than the real one. What if he didn't love her? Her words came slowly. "I think you must know why." He waited for her to go on, so she whispered, "I love you, Pete."

He drew her close. "Can you forgive me?"

She nodded as much as was possible. "Of course."

"I went to see Allyson after we parted in the street." He hugged her yet more closely as she started to draw away but then must have thought better of that and released her. She straightened on the couch, confused, and he didn't touch her as he continued. "I hadn't seen her for a couple of weeks and decided it was time. . . ."

Her eyelids closed in their effort to hide pain, but then reopened.

Pete's voice went on. "That we straighten out exactly where we stand. As I told you, we've been friends for many years and in all honesty there have been times I considered marrying her."

More pain—sharp, continuing.

"But that was for all the wrong reasons, Tess—getting along well, having fun together, knowing and doing things with the same people—that sort of thing. When I thought of spending the rest of my life with her...having her be the mother of my children. . .coming home to her every day...knowing she doesn't have a commitment to Christ, which should have been my first consideration—I just couldn't do it."

He drew in a deep breath and let it out very slowly. "I went to see her Sunday and told her this. She accused me of letting you come between us, which is logical from her point of view, but I explained how relieved I'd been to get this teaching position, and that was before I knew you existed."

Was he telling Tess that Allyson didn't really matter to him?

"I said I had needed space and time to sort things out. And she asked if I'd done this. I said I had. I was sure, now, that we could be nothing more than friends.

"She let me know that was unacceptable. . .that it was marriage or nothing."

He got up and walked around the coffee table, hands stuffed into his pockets as he faced her. "So, it's nothing."

Tess looked up at him, this wonderful man whom she loved more than life itself. And yet he had still never said or done anything to give reason for believing he loved her. Oh yes, they had hugged on the rooftop and he had held her here on the couch a minute ago, but. . . . "How do you . . .feel about that?" she asked into the silence.

"Good."

"Somewhat. . .empty?" She had to know.

"Not empty. More like. . .free. Free to speak to you of things I've kept bottled up so long. Free to tell you that I love you far beyond what I've ever felt for anyone else. Free to hold you in my arms and kiss you—if you'll let me after the beastly way I've treated you."

"Then," she stood up, happiness in her eyes to match that in her heart, "why are you way over there?"

Tess met him halfway, trusting her kisses and hugs to show her otherwise inexpressible joy. The heartache, loneliness, and longing were over. *He loves me. He loves me!*

The tuna and tossed salads they made together and ate

at the kitchen table were flavored by the zest of their newly expressed love and were enjoyed more than anything they might have ordered in the finest restaurant.

"I'm so glad I went to Florida with you," she said, leaning over to kiss him again as she placed a dish of ice cream on the table before him.

He tousled her hair. "Me, too. I liked you before. . .I loved you then."

"It took you long enough to let me know," she murmured, remembering her insecurity.

"I had to be sure. To be positive this wasn't a. . . rebounding from Allyson. And that it really was what I thought—a forever, till-death-do-us-part kind of love."

Later, he told her, "I want you to know it hasn't been easy for me all these weeks, either, Tess. I was miserable much of the time, afraid if I didn't speak up I'd lose you to Pastor Jim."

Even though she herself had suspected Pastor Jim might be interested, she hadn't realized that Pete would think such a thing. He added, "Pastor Jim's such a great guy I was afraid God, knowing he needs a helpmate like you in the parsonage, might have that in His plans."

She couldn't help feeling a little glad that he had suffered also. But she asked softly, "And you, Pete, do you also need a helpmate like me?"

His passionate kiss was the immediate answer that left no doubts in her mind or heart.

The answering machine at the parsonage indicated that

Pastor Jim expected to be back from his meeting around nine. Tess and Pete drove to her father's to share their news and on the way back stopped at Molly's. She welcomed them into her home with, "So what's new with you young folks?"

"There is something—something wonderful," Tess began.

Molly unerringly read the beaming happiness on their faces and wrapped her arms around them. "You're getting married! I've been praying about this every single day, but then I'd see you sitting alone and coming and going separately. I was beginning to wonder if I was wrong."

"Had you given up on us yet?" Pete inquired.

"I couldn't do that."

Pastor Jim, when they found him, was even less surprised. "I've known how you felt since those days in Florida, Tess. Your climbing that ladder and working on the roof with Pete told me the love you had for him was sufficient to cast out long-lasting fears.

"And, Pete, I would have had to be blind not to recognize your pain and what you were suffering as she coped with her asthma. And how you admired her. You couldn't have been that solicitous and caring without a personal reason."

Pete started to say something but Pastor Jim went on. "So I've been praying along with Molly for the resolution of whatever was keeping you from acknowledging your love. I'm delighted you're planning for the future together."

They began making arrangements for a simple wedding to be held at the end of a Sunday morning worship service. "Neither of us wants a lot of pomp or extravagant show," she told Pastor Jim. "We'd like our marriage to be a worshipful, blessed experience with those we know and treasure here in the church. And our folks and Aunt Freddie and a few others, of course."

Prior to that, they would have their six counseling sessions with Pastor Jim. "We don't know yet which of our apartments we'll live in when we're married," she said. "Logically, it should be Pete's, as he has the longer lease—"

"But she still hasn't seen it," Pete finished her sentence.

They received Pastor Jim's blessing and then left for Pete's apartment. He unlocked but hesitated before opening the door. "It's a bachelor pad, Tess."

Her eyebrows raised in the question he responded to with, "I'm not a housekeeper, I'm afraid. I just live here."

She smiled up at him, saying nothing.

"It's sort of. . .," he began as he reluctantly turned the knob.

"It's home, Pete. We've been together in some awful places, remember? But wherever you are, Florida, or here, or anywhere—if I'm with you, I'll be home."

His arm drew her close. They went through the doorway—together.

Never had it been so marvelous to be "home."

A Letter To Our Readers

Dear Reader:

In order that we might better contribute to your reading enjoyment, we would appreciate your taking a few minutes to respond to the following questions. When completed, please return to the following:

Karen Carroll, Editor
Heartsong Presents
P.O. Box 719
Uhrichsville, Ohio 44683

1. Did you enjoy reading *A Place to Call Home*?
   ☐ Very much. I would like to see more books
      by this author!
   ☐ Moderately
      I would have enjoyed it more if _____

   _____

2. Are you a member of *Heartsong Presents*? Yes   No
   If no, where did you purchase this book? _____

   _____

3. What influenced your decision to purchase
   this book? (Circle those that apply.)

Cover	Back cover copy
Title	Friends
Publicity	Other _____

4. On a scale from 1 (poor) to 10 (superior), please rate the following elements.

    ___Heroine   ___Plot

    ___Hero   ___Inspirational theme

    ___Setting   ___Secondary characters

5. What settings would you like to see covered in *Heartsong Presents* books?

_____

_____

6. What are some inspirational themes you would like to see treated in future books?_____

_____

_____

7. Would you be interested in reading other *Heartsong Presents* titles?   Yes   No

8. Please circle your age range:

Under 18	18-24	25-34
35-45	46-55	Over 55

9. How many hours per week do you read? _____

Name _____

Occupation _____

Address _____

City _____ State _____ Zip _____

add a little *MYSTERY* to your romance!

TWO GREAT INSPIRATIONAL ROMANCES WITH JUST A TOUCH OF MYSTERY
BY MARLENE J. CHASE

_____*The Other Side of Silence*—Anna Durham finds a purpose for living in the eyes of a needy child and a reason to love in the eyes of a lonely physician...but first the silence of secrets must be broken. HP6 BHSB-07 $2.95.

_____*This Trembling Cup*—A respite on a plush Wisconsin resort may just be the thing for Angie Carlson's burn-out—or just the beginning of a devious plot unraveling and the promise of love. HP5 BHSB-05 $2.95.

LOVE A GREAT LOVE STORY?
Introducing Heartsong Presents —
Your Inspirational Book Club

Heartsong Presents Christian romance reader's service will provide you with four never before published romance titles every month! In fact, your books will be mailed to you at the same time advance copies are sent to book reviewers. You'll preview each of these new and unabridged books before they are released to the general public.

These books are filled with the kind of stories you have been longing for—stories of courtship, chivalry, honor, and virtue. Strong characters and riveting plot lines will make you want to read on and on. Romance is not dead, and each of these romantic tales will remind you that Christian faith is still the vital ingredient in an intimate relationship filled with true love and honest devotion.

Sign up today to receive your first set. Send no money now. We'll bill you only $9.97 post-paid with your shipment. Then every month you'll automatically receive the latest four "hot off the press" titles for the same low post-paid price of $9.97. That's a savings of 50% off the $4.95 cover price. When you consider the exaggerated shipping charges of other book clubs, your savings are even greater!

THERE IS NO RISK—you may cancel at any time without obligation. And if you aren't completely satisfied with any selection, return it for an immediate refund.

TO JOIN, just complete the coupon below, mail it today, and get ready for hours of wholesome entertainment.

Now you can curl up, relax, and enjoy some great reading full of the warmhearted spirit of romance.